George Lansing Raymond

Cecil the Seer

George Lansing Raymond

Cecil the Seer

ISBN/EAN: 9783337334758

Printed in Europe, USA, Canada, Australia, Japan

Cover: Foto ©Andreas Hilbeck / pixelio.de

More available books at **www.hansebooks.com**

CECIL THE SEER

A DRAMA OF THE SOUL

BY

WALTER WARREN

AUTHOR OF "COLUMBUS THE DISCOVERER," "THE AZTECS," ETC.

BOSTON
ARENA PUBLISHING COMPANY
COPLEY SQUARE
1894

PLACE AND TIME.

ACT FIRST : In a Southern " Border State " of the American Union, a little before the War for Secession. An evening party at the home of the Cecils. *Scene :* A large hall with glimpses beyond it of a parlor and a porch.

ACT SECOND : *Scenes First and Third :* Interior of a sick chamber. *Scene Second :* A grove representing the surroundings of a dream or trance.

ACT THIRD : In a Northern " Border State " just at the opening of the War for Secession. *Scene First :* The interior of the home of Freeman and Celia ; *Scene Second :* A village green in front of Freeman's house, at one side of which the porch of his house is visible.

CHARACTERS.

CECIL.
Professor in a College, a Candidate for the highest Judicial Office of the State, to be appointed by its Governor and confirmed by its Senate. Also a particular friend and the instructor of Celia.

KRAFT.
Head Politician of the ruling party of the State, and a particular friend of Madam Cecil. Celia has been the adopted daughter of his deceased wife.

FREEMAN.
A young Law Student, friend of Cecil and Celia, and in love with Faith Hycher.

BLAVER.
Religious Exhorter, and Head of the Prohibition party of the State. Particular friend of Miss Primwood.

FATHER HYCHER.
Head of the Church party of the State who wish to obtain a division of the School Fund. Uncle of Faith Hycher, and particular friend of Widow Hycher, his sister-in-law.

LOWE.
A Quaker, representing a syndicate of railway monopolists who are pushing a plan for appropriating and improving a part of the chief city of the State.

JEM.
A colored servant.

CELIA.   Adopted daughter of deceased wife of
                    Kraft. Pupil and particular friend of
                    Cecil and Freeman.

CECILIA.   An idealized Celia, appearing throughout
                    the dream in Act Second.—To be acted
                    by the same one who acts Celia.

MADAM CECIL.   Wife of Cecil, particular friend of Kraft.

FAITH HYCHER.   In love with Freeman, niece of Father
                    Hycher and step-daughter of Widow
                    Hycher.

MISS PRIMWOOD.   Principal of a Female Seminary, particular
                    friend of Blaver.

WIDOW HYCHER.   Step-mother of Faith Hycher, particular
                    friend of her brother-in-law, Father
                    Hycher.

MADAM LOWE.   Quakeress, wife of Lowe.

MILLY.   A colored servant.

*A Physician, Choristers, Promenaders, Dancers, Populace,
Ruffians, Detectives, Militia, etc.*

CECIL, THE SEER.

ACT FIRST.

SCENE: *An evening party at the home of the Cecils. A large hall or parlor. Backing at the Right, extending diagonally across the stage, a wide doorway, beyond which is a glimpse of a porch and garden. Further forward on the Right, a small table about which are three chairs. Further forward still, between the place of the Right Second and the Right Front Entrances, a bay window containing a sofa, and apparently hiding those seated upon it from the view of others in the hall. Backing at the Left, extending diagonally across the stage, a wide doorway, beyond which is a glimpse of another room.*

ENTRANCES: *Right Upper, through the doorway; Right Third, through a long window open from the floor up; and Right Front, through a doorway. Left Upper, through a doorway, and Left Second, through a doorway.*

> *Curtain rising discloses* FREEMAN *and* FATHER
> HYCHER *sitting in the bay window, and
> couples walking to and fro upon the
> stage.*

FATHER HYCHER.   My standards are the standards
  of the world,

FREEMAN.   I know it.

FATHER H.   You were questioning—— .

FREEMAN.   Their truth.

FATHER H.   (*slowly and sarcastically*).
  Your name is Freeman.

FREEMAN.   It defines me, yes.

FATHER H.   You think fidelity to man can grow
  From germs of infidelity to God?
  You think that questioning the forms men most
  Esteem, proves high esteem for men themselves?
  You think in one that's wed, or vowed to wed,
  To love a third one proves pure love for all?

FREEMAN.   That all depends on what he does.

FATHER H.   And that?

FREEMAN.   On what he is.   Why ask these things
  of me?—
  And here?

FATHER H.   Why should I not?   One sees so much
  In scenes like this!

FREEMAN.   Oh no!—You mean so little.
  The forms we see are puppets of a play,
  A dull play too! Though seek what pulls the
    string,

'Tis dull no longer.   Soon a button breaks,
A veil falls off——
FATHER H.   Too bad to hope for that!
FREEMAN.   Too bad, if lives be bad!   If not, too
   good!
Some things that on the outside seem profane,
Upon the inside may be sacred.
FATHER H.   Ah?
FREEMAN,   The converse too is true.
FATHER H. (*haughtily*).
                You mean to say?—
        (*Music starts.*)
FREEMAN (*rising, as does* FATHER HYCHER.)
   That all should watch the play, and not forget
   They're part of it themselves.
FATHER H. (*looking toward Right*).   I see I'm wanted.
Exit—Right Front—after bowing to Freeman,
        FATHER H. (FREEMAN *moves toward the
        Right Upper Entrance.   The following
        chorus is sung to the accompaniment of a
        piano apparently in the rooms beyond the
        Left Upper Entrance.   During the sing-
        ing certain of those upon the stage, or enter-
        ing from its various entrances, dance to
        the music*).

We live but for bubbles, and those who know
The way of the world their bubbles will blow.
Ay, all but who 're willing their doings should be
No more than are drops in an infinite sea,

Will blow them, and show them, till, by and by,
They fill and float to the air on high;
Hoho! hoho! and the world will thus
See how big a bubble can come from us.

We live but for bubbles that grow and glow
The bigger and brighter the more we blow;
And, borne on the breath of the breeze around
Wherever the tides of the time are bound,
There is nothing of earth or of heaven in sight
But they'll image it all in a rainbow light;
Hoho! hoho! and the world will thus
See how bright a bubble can come from us.

We live but for bubbles a-dance in the blast,
But who can tell how long they will last?
So swell your cheeks, and puff, and fan,
And make the most of them while you can,
For if ever the breath in them fail, they will pop,
And only be drizzles to dry as they drop;
Ho-ho! ho-ho! and the world will thus
Be done with the bubbles that came from us.

> *Enter—Right   Upper — during the singing,*
> FAITH.   *She meets* FREEMAN *and, after a*
> *time, they sit in the bay window at the*
> *Right.*
> *Exeunt—at different Entrances—the dancers or*
> *singers.*

FAITH.   This night seems like a *fête* in fairy-land.
That singing proves it so.   I like to see
Our Cecil circled by the people singing.
FREEMAN.   You note its meaning then?

FAITH. What?

FREEMAN. Cecil-worship.

FAITH. And worship in the interest men pay
For worth when they can get it—justly due
To men of principle.

FREEMAN. And how of women?
'Tis Madam Cecil is the priestess here.
She'll take the fee. He's but the puppet-idol.

FAITH. How so?

FREEMAN. Our foremost judgeship must be filled.

FAITH. And what of that?

FREEMAN. It is a high position.
And she, who's always looking up, has seen it.

FAITH. That may be ; but you spoke of worship.

FREEMAN. Why,
If there's an idol's niche left tenantless,
The one all worship is the one all want there.

FAITH. Oh yes !—and Madam Cecil——

FREEMAN. Drawing hither
The undirected flow of current thought,
Though little rills, may find them, all together,
Enough to float the bark of her ambition.
You see this house—and she herself—are gems.
For setting, gems need gold. Her husband earns
By teaching in the college, at the most,
No gold to spare ; and, even did she hope,
From her own managing. no perquisites——

FAITH. What perquisites ?

FREEMAN. The kind that make us call

A public man " His Honor," lest the world
Might fail to recognize it, if not labeled.

FAITH.　Will Cecil get the place?

FREEMAN.　　　　　　　　The governor
May nominate him ; but the senators
Can scarcely be expected to confirm,
Without some reason not upon the surface,
A man so young and inexperienced.

FAITH.　He's worthy of it.

FREEMAN.　　　　　Worthy !—What is worth
With those that she will try to get to push him?
Their favors must be paid for.　Most have suits
They sue for in the law courts.　Think you
　Cecil,
An upright, downright and straightforward nature,
Will twist and smirk with twenty different faces
The twenty different ways that these would have
　him?

FAITH.　It were a brilliant chance !

FREEMAN.　　　　　Yes, far too brilliant
For moths to meet with, and escape a scorching.
He suns in higher light.　'T will not daze him.

FAITH (*looking toward the left*).
There's Madam Cecil now—

FREEMAN (*rising*).　And angels too,
They say, draw near us when we talk of them.

FAITH (*also rising*).　With her comes Kraft.

FREEMAN.　　　　　He's ruler of his party,—
Controls the governor.

FAITH.   Ah ! And Cecil, then,—
Are he and Kraft such friends ?
FREEMAN.   No ; she and Kraft,
A man she's deluged with such flattery
That his half drowned, asphyxied reason raves
Past all resisting her.   Nor that alone.
I've heard he means to seat that son of his
In Cecil's present chair.   Your men that rule,
When others hold the place that they would fill,
Tramp an inferior, and push off an equal ;
But when the selfish scheme they brew is spoiled
By one above them,—why, they 're left no option;
But, like a cover, they must lift him higher.
So, by their very righteousness, you see
The righteous force their foes to do them justice.
    *Exeunt—Right Front—*FREEMAN *and* FAITH.
    *Enter—Left Upper—*KRAFT *with* MADAM CECIL.
MADAM C.   Your charming son—
KRAFT.   Gains charms from you who say that—
MADAM C.   Has such a noble brow, and eyes, and
    manner.
KRAFT.   Yes ; he is like his—mother.
MADAM C.   Why, my friend,
His mien, his manner are as like to yours,
As ever were the echoes of a wood
To singing of a woodsman.
KRAFT.   Oh, you flatter !
MADAM C.   And pardon, if I add both have their
    music.

KRAFT. No, no; but Madam Cecil, you do
    flatter!

MADAM C. Not half so much, my good friend, as
    your mirror,

When you but face—

KRAFT (*looking at her intently*).

              And find it very bright?—

But now, about my son : I think of course—

MADAM C. What I think. Do we ever disagree?

KRAFT. I wish your husband could be led—

MADAM C.   You think

He cannot then?

KRAFT.   Why that depends—

MADAM C. ,   On whom?—

A good judge is a man whose judgments you

Approve.

KRAFT (*bowing to her*).

    Thanks for your interest.

*Enter—Left Second—*MR. BLAVER *with* MISS PRIM-
WOOD.

MADAM C. (*continuing to* KRAFT).

            Why that

Becomes me,—does it not? I've heard you
    say

I always do, as well as wear, the thing

That seems becoming;—and the principal

(*touching* KRAFT *with her fan; then pointing it toward herself.*)

Should always draw its interest. Not so?—

(*turning to speak to* Miss Primwood *and* Blaver,
    who carries a pamphlet in his hand.)
Miss Primwood, ah ! Good-evening—You too,
    Deacon :
(*All bow.* Kraft *talks aside to* Miss Primwood.
    Madam Cecil *continues to* Blaver, *tapping
    his pamphlet with her fan.*)
We've read your little prohibition tracts.
Blaver.   Yes?—Thanks.—But, as you say, they're
    very little.
Madam C.   The smallest diamond in this ring I
    wear
Is better for my humble, human use,
Than a whole world of dust whirled in a star
Set in an orbit out beyond my reach.
Blaver.   If, in some humble way, my tracts do
    good—
Madam C.   The littlest bird-track, sometimes, in
    the sand
May make one think of wings flown out of sight.
Blaver.   If only mine would—wings of progress,
    say.
Madam C.   Ah, but your cause is right.
Blaver.   Yes, all our pleas
Are based upon religion.   Yet you know
The lower courts are hostile.
    *Exeunt—Left—*Miss Primwood *and* Kraft.
Madam C.   Right must win.
Blaver.   You think so ?—The professor too ?—

MADAM C. (*assuming an air of disparagement*).

Come, come ;
. No man should anchor trust in such as he,
Why your opponents never——
BLAVER (*eagerly*).

Would support him ?—
They would not?
MADAM C.   Would ?—how could they ? Do you know,
'Twas only last night, when some friends were here
And talking of the governorship, he said
Our next might be a prohibitionist.
BLAVER (*greatly pleased, rubbing his hands*).
Is that so ?   Really !—Is that so ?   Why, why !—
MADAM C.   (*tapping him with her fan*). You may be governor yet.   You may, you may !—
*Enter—Left Second—*FATHER HYCHER *with* WIDOW HYCHER.
(MADAM C., *noticing them, says aside,*).
But there comes Father Hycher—
(*insinuatingly to* BLAVER).

Do you think
A man, religious truly, would not stand
Upon a platform based upon religion ?
(MADAM C. *and* BLAVER *bow to* FATHER H. *and* WIDOW HYCHER. BLAVER *talks aside to* WIDOW H. *and, with her, presently, exits at the Left—*MADAM C. *continues talking to* FATHER HYCHER).

You act like saints we read of in the legends,
With holy air about you. As you entered,
Our thoughts turned toward religion.

FATHER H.   Ah ?—with mine !—
I saw you at the church, the other day.

MADAM C.   I heard the Father was to preach—

FATHER H.   And came ?—

MADAM C.   To be a worshipper.

FATHER H.   You think perhaps,
That we make less of preaching than of praise.

MADAM C.   Now, honestly, I do admire your
form.

FATHER H.   I like to see you give it countenance.
But, really, Madam Cecil, you are right.
We must have form :—all eyes, ears, crave it so.
The only question, as I say, is this—
Which form is *the*——

MADAM C.   The form the most emphatic,
One might call *the* form.

FATHER H.   Right, just right again !-
In schools, asylums, prisons, everywhere
That souls should be impressed——

MADAM C.   There one should use
The most impressive form.

FATHER H.   Why, this is strange !
Just what I told your husband !

MADAM C. (*laughing significantly*).   So you've
learned
A woman's thoughts are echoes ; and she echoes

2

The thoughts that have been nearest to the heart
To which she stands the nearest.

FATHER H. No—but I—
How could I think my words had had such
weight?

MADAM C. Words are a currency that owe their
worth
Less to their substance, often, than their source.

FATHER H. Your husband, then, you think——

MADAM C. (*with an implied suggestion*).
A man that knows
Enough to judge a beaker by its brand.

FATHER H. I did not think I had such influence.

MADAM C. Nor does the sun. It never thinks at all;
Yet keeps the whole world whirling—by its
light?—
No, no,—by its position.

FATHER H. If the courts
Would only recognize that, and the wrong
Of taxing our schools to support a rule
From which our own religion is ruled out—

MADAM C. And on your side are many senators?—
And they confirm the judges?

FATHER H. What of that?

MADAM C. Why, Father, sometimes I have played
at whist;
And when my partner holds the cards that win——

*Enter—Right Front—*FREEMAN *and* FAITH, *presently seating themselves in the bay window.*

*Enter—Left Second—*LOWE *carrying a map-*
like plan of streets, parks, etc. Other
GENTLEMEN *enter with him. All sur-*
round MADAM C.

FATHER II. (*to* MADAM C.).

What then?

MADAM C.   Then I play low.   That's whist.

FATHER II.   Ha ! ha !

FREEMAN (*to* FAITH).

See Madam Cecil.   How her ribboned form

Bends o'er the black coats !—like a bow of
   promise

Above thick cloud-banks.   Each one thinks he sees

Those of his own cloth fly at Cecil's bidding

Like crows where grows but shall not grow a
   harvest.

Oh, to be popular, just let one be

Abulge with promise, pledging everything.

Till time present him his protested bills,

The world will fawn and paw him like a hound

To do his bidding.   Promise is a flea :

It makes us itch ; but fools us, would we catch it.

MADAM C. (*looking over* LOWE'S *plans*).

This line here is the river bank,—not so ?

LOWE.   And here the railway ; and the park is here,
   And here the church (*pointing*).

MADAM C.   The church ?

LOWE.   You know with me

Religion is the chief consideration.

MADAM C.   I know; but you're a friend?

LOWE.   The company
Are world's folk,—will not build a meeting. So
We would not quarrel with them : we build this.

MADAM C.   Yes.   How considerate !

LOWE.   'Tis my wish to be so.

MADAM C.   But no one lives here yet ?

LOWE.   In time some will.

MADAM C.   And, for their future good, you build
the church ?

*Exit—Left Upper—*FATHER HYCHER.

LOWE.   Yet some do not approve it.

MADAM C.   Is there doubt
Of your success ?

LOWE.   Oh no—not if the courts
Remove the injunction of the district's owners.

MADAM C.   But that will follow.   As my husband
says,
The corner stones of monumental deeds
Must always crush some worms ; and plans like
these
(*laughing good-naturedly*)
Are monumental—even in their size !
Suppose we find a table for them here.
(*gesturing toward the Left.*)
*Exeunt—Left Second—*MADAM C., LOWE *and
other* GENTLEMEN.

FREEMAN (*to* FAITH).
This is the foremost swindle of them all,—

A syndicate that steals the river bank ;
Then taxes doubly those they steal it from
For what is left them.   But the abuse is old.
Where thrived ambition yet, but strove to build
Itself a monument by heaping up
That which, when lost, made hollow all about it !
How many castle-towns I've seen in Europe,
Where every graceful touch in breadth and height
That formed the great hall's pride, appeared out-
      lined
As if by shadowy finger-prints of force
That snatched all from the low lands at its base !
But look you—there is Cecil, and with Celia.
      (*pointing toward Left Upper Entrance.*)
How   indiscreet !   She's   ward,   you   know,   of
      Kraft,
Who only can make Cecil judge ; and Kraft
Hates Celia, treats her like a slave, they say.
FAITH.   Why so ?
FREEMAN.   He has his reasons.
FAITH (*rising*).   Do you know them ?
      (FREEMAN *rising and shrugging his shoulders.*)
'Twas said that you admired her too ?
FREEMAN.   I did.
      Before my eyes met you——
FAITH.   This never can be.
My uncle's honor and mine own are pledged.
FREEMAN.   But honor helping none and harming
      self,

Need never serve the body of a vow
From which the life to which it vowed has flown.
Exeunt—Right First—FAITH *and* FREEMAN.
Enter—Left Upper Entrance—CELIA *and* CECIL.
CECIL.   Must leave off study, Celia?
CELIA.   So it seems.
CECIL.   To be their brightest, minds need bur-
        nishing;
    And earth needs all the light that we can give it.
CELIA.   I know—were I not so opposed—then,
        too,
    I'm but a woman.   What can woman do?
CECIL.   Do, Celia, do?
CELIA.   Why, yes—what starts with her?
CECIL.   No matter what.   Men sow the seed, you
        think.
    How could it grow, were it to find no soil?
    You've seen the crystal globes clairvoyants use,
    And think they see the heavens in?—Some
        women
    Have souls like that.   One faces them to find
    His thoughts divine, himself akin to God.
CELIA.   If that be woman's nature——
CECIL.   It is not,
    Till polished in the friction of the schools,
    Which some think needless; but where woman's
        mind
    Has never been made bright, the thoughts of men
    Will never flash for it.

CELIA. The sun may find
Its image in the dullest pool.
CECIL. To be
Too modest, is we lag behind, and break
God's lines, who ranks us right.
CELIA. But eyes, they say,
Made free to roam round all the world of thought
Find views too strange——
CECIL. To those this side of it?—
Who envy what they cannot see themselves?
CELIA. They say they hate what does not aid
religion.
CECIL. Aid whose, and what?—their own?—and
are they sure
They do not make themselves their lord, forsooth,
Because they wish to lord it over others?
CELIA. It may have been my fault—I had a dream—
CECIL. You're blamed for dreaming then?
CELIA. No, but I told it.
CECIL. Another Joseph!—indiscreet, I see.
You should have known we all at heart are Tar-
tars ;
And value most the beauty of the spirit,
When, like the Tartar's daughter, it is veiled.—
And yet, if unveiled once, why not for me?
CELIA. 'Twas but a whim. I thought, and said I
thought
That, if a soul must live hereafter, why,
It must have lived before.—You know the Christ

Did not rebuke the throng that said some thought
Elias had returned ; but, in an age
When all believed it might be, said 'twas true.
And then our creed—Where can it come to pass, —
The body's resurrection ?

CECIL.   Where?

CELIA.   Where but
In that new earth of Hebrew prophecies ?—
Which would have but misled, had those that
    heard
Not had it in their power themselves to be
Restored to life in that restored estate.

CECIL.   Seems life so bright then ?—You would live
    it over ?

CELIA.   No, no; so sad that I would solve its
    reason.
If we have lived before, we all are born
In spheres to which our own deeds destine us.

CECIL.   Not Adam's ?

CELIA.   Each one may have been an Adam ;
And therefore made a slave now.

CECIL.   You a slave?

CELIA.   I must tell some one—let me tell it you :
To Kraft, whose wife, ere death, was more to me
Than mother, I'm a waif.

CECIL.   But others prize you.
A jewel is not judged by its surroundings.

CELIA.   And yet a jewel might be cheaply bartered
By one who did not prize it.

CECIL. Bartered ?—You——

CELIA. Note my complexion—who think you my
mother ?—

CECIL. What, what ?—Kraft never claimed you as a
slave ?

CELIA. Nor will, perhaps ; but he has threatened it ;
And even the suggestion of this here—

CECIL But what's his object?

CELIA. I alone have seen
The writings that were left him by his wife,—
Her wish to free her slaves——

CECIL. Oh, what a worm
Is greed for gold ! Did ever human fruitage
Turn into rot but it had gnawed the core ?—
Was there a will ?

(CELIA *nods slightly*.)

You are in danger, yes.

CELIA. A wretch has come, as vile as he is
ugly ;
And if I were the charmer of a snake,
· I could not shrink from touch more horrible.

CECIL. And what of him ?

CELIA. Why, I must go with him ;
Indeed, have been forbidden to come here.

CECIL. To-night ?

CELIA. To-night.

CECIL. Must marry him ?

CELIA. Nay, worse.
He needs, or says he needs, a housekeeper.

CECIL. Why, Celia, this is monstrous! By what means
Would Kraft enforce his will?
CELIA.   By force itself;
And what he deems my ignorance.
CECIL.   Tell me, child,
Has Kraft good reasons?
CELIA.   If he has?
CECIL.   Why, then,
By your white soul, and by the work of Christ,
In spite of threatened storms with thunderbolts
As thick as bristling blades in a bayonet charge,
I'll stand between you and the coming danger.
CELIA. I thank you, friend; but no; your race is mine.
But 'twill take time to prove it.
CECIL.   Who meanwhile
Will guard you?
CELIA.   Yes—who will?
CECIL.   That son of Kraft?
CELIA. He's such a villain, that his daintiest deed
Of courtesy's a counterfeited coin
With which he chaffers and intends to cheat.
If I were drowning, I would dread to grasp
The hand he stretched to draw me near himself.
Better to die at once, when washed and clean,
Than catch contagion and live on defiled.
CECIL. You must remain at my house.
                *Enter—Left second—*KRAFT.

KRAFT (*aside*). Celia here?

CELIA. (*noticing* KRAFT).

I—I—have an engagement. I must go.

*Exit—Left Upper—*CELIA.

KRAFT (*to* CECIL).

I interrupt.

CECIL (*to* KRAFT). 'Tis nothing.—She was saying
That you desired to have her stop her studies.

KRAFT. Yes, she must win her bread.

CECIL. Of course, but how?

KRAFT. That's my affair.

CECIL. Why, no; not wholly,—is it?
Let me relieve you of the charge of her.
I'll take it on myself. In two years' time,
She'll teach, and pay us back—with interest.

KRAFT (*sarcastically*). Perhaps; but, by the way,
now, that you speak
Of teaching, there is no one named, I think,
For your professorship, in case you leave it.

CECIL. 'Tis not left yet.

KRAFT. But may be, if you wish.
If not, too, there are more professorships;
And if so, there's my son.

CECIL. I see. No doubt
His claims would have fair hearing.

KRAFT. But if you
Could recommend him——

CECIL. That would pass for little;
I know so little of him.

KRAFT.   But your word——
CECIL.   Would, like a bank-note, quickly lose its
     worth
   Were nothing stored behind it, to make true
   The storage it bespeaks.
KRAFT.   Oh yes, I've found
   The men most praised for judgment are the men
   Most echoing others' judgments.   Thus, forsooth,
   They make their own appear approved by all.
CECIL.   Not so with me !   Has he experience
   In teaching ?
KRAFT.   He has knowledge.
CECIL.   For a teacher,
   A knowledge of mere books does not suffice ;
   He needs a knowledge too of human nature ;
   And sympathy, to make his teaching welcome ;
   And fire, to make it felt ; and tact and skill,
   To aim and temper it for others' needs ;
   And modesty to keep his own acquirements
   In strictest servitude to their demands ;
   And dignity that comes from honoring truth,
   To crown its servant as the student's master.
   What think you ?   Has he these ?
KRAFT.   He's had no chance
   To show——
CECIL.   Then why not test him where a failure
   Would not be trumpeted ?   A man's best friend
   Will bid him wait for honor till he earn it.
   Amid earth's envious crush of frenzied greed,

'Tis not a kindness, pushing to the front
One who is not a leader. Zealous forms
That crowd him there, may tramp him under foot.

Enter—Left Second—A GENTLEMAN, *beckoning to*
KRAFT.

KRAFT (*noticing the* GENTLEMAN, *and bowing to him,*
and also to CECIL).

Thanks, thanks. I will remember what you say.

*Exeunt—Left Second—*KRAFT *and* GENTLEMAN.

CECIL (*alone*).

If Celia judged him right, his son shall get
No honor which my justice can deny him.
Humph! Prudence hints I've ruined all my
 hopes.
Let go then! 'Tis a simple question this :—
Shall I play slave to Kraft, Lowe, Hycher,
 Blaver ?—
Sell them the justice that is in my soul
To seem to deal out justice for the state ?—
No ; better be God's creature though a worm,
Than theirs, though they had power to make me
 king !

*Exit—Left Upper—*CECIL.

Dance music. Enter at the different entrances,
dancers in couples or in sets. At last,
those nearest the Left Upper Entrance
beckon to the others, and all, as if suddenly
called away, exeunt at the Left Upper
Entrance.

*Enter—Left Second Entrance—*JEM, *carrying
a tray with plates and refreshments on it.
He looks at dancers, then crosses the stage
to the bay window, where, meeting* MILLY,
he places the tray on the seat.

*Enter—Right Front Entrance—*MILLY, *carrying a tray with glasses containing iced tea
She too places her tray on a seat in the bay
window.*

JEM (*looking at departing dancers*).

Dey's all gone wheah de tables is, I reckon,
          (*looking at Milly*)
De white folks hab deir shadders.

MILLY.   An' dey dance

Behin' de white folks' back.
         (JEM *and* MILLY *dance.*)

Jem (*stretching his hand to take* MILLY'S).

           Oh, heah! come heah!

MILLY (*drawing back her hand*).

No, no, you don't.

JEM (*looking sharply at her hand, which she keeps
clenched*).

          Now tell me what you got

In dat black hollah dah.

MILLY (*jerking her hand away*).

           Jes' what you habn't.

JEM. Come, come, now, Milly. Lawd ob all de stahs!

Dis heah's a patch ob his own pitchy sky,
An' hol's a stah in dah. Whose am it, hey?

MILLY. Whose? Mine.

JEM. You'll catch it — livin' deed o' darkness!

MILLY (*throwing an ear-ring from one hand into the other*).

Dey'll hab to catch dis fust.

JEM. Come, you knows, Milly,
Dat I'll not gib you way. Say, whah 'd you get it?

MILLY. Why, on de floah.

JEM. Who dwopt it off 'um den?

MILLY. Why, dem as owes us twenty times so much
As dat 'ill fetch us.
(*Shaking the ear-ring at* JEM.)

JEM. Ah, dat's right.

MILLY (*putting ear-ring in her pocket*).
Ay, ay,
An' doin' right.

JEM. Except dat you's not dancin'
(JEM *and* MILLY *dance*).
Heah, heah, now, heah an' heah!

MILLY (*stopping, and gesturing to* JEM *who keeps on dancing*).
Now, Jem, stay put.

JEM. For why?

MILLY. Dey'll fin' us out.

JEM. Ugh, dey can't see us.

MILLY. Ole missus 's allers houndin' roun', you know,
To fin' de niggah.

(*Moving, and gesturing toward the bay window.*)
Dah. Sit down,

(MILLY *sits in the bay window.* JEM *takes refreshments and passes them to her*).

JEM. An' take
De crums dat's fallen from de rich man's table.
Dat's scripter.

(JEM *sits down. Both eat.*)

Look heah, Milly, say——

MILLY. Say what?

JEM. I likes dis cake. It's sweet, and yet, you knows,
Dis dahkey's lips would like anoder cake.

(*Puckering lips, as if to kiss her.*)

MILLY. Oh, you go home

JEM (*looking out of the window*).

No ; it am cold out dah.

MILLY. Den let it shake you! you's got one wife now.

JEM. Not one! De las' one, Dinah, 's sold, you know.

MILLY. Law sakes! I hadn't heahd o' dat.

JEM. She'm gone
Gone like the dark cloud when the night. am come.
I'll nebah see her moah.

MILLY. Jem dat am sad.

JEM. An' you don't reckon dis Jem's meant to be
A gem widout a settin ?'

MILLY. Dah's de white folks.

*Enter—Left Upper—*BLAVER *and* MISS PRIM-
WOOD.—MILLY *and* JEM *rise, taking their
trays.*

JEM. Well, dey don't reckon so neider.

MILLY. What dey reckon,
Dey showed by sellin' Dinah.

JEM. What you reckon——

MILLY. Is all de numbers ob your wives !
(*bowing to* JEM.)

JEM. You can't.

*Exeunt—Right Front Entrance—*MILLY *and* JEM
hurriedly.

MISS PRIMWOOD (*catching a glimpse of them, and
holding up her hands*).
There's no religion, none—I tell you none.
Men are not solemnized as once they were.

BLAVER. No, they are sodomized. You say you
saw
(*pointing toward the Left.*)
In Cecil's hand, a reddish-colored dram ?

MISS PRIMWOOD. It might have been——

BLAVER. To those who saw it drunk
It looked, at least, like liquor. He was not
Avoiding the appearances of evil.
He's not the man I thought—no proper mate
For Madam Cecil. She——

MISS PRIMWOOD. You think so, eh ?——
Men never will know women. This is hers—

3

Her party—making those not thirsty drink,
And eat, when they've no appetite,—and dance,
When, prudence knows, they ought to be in bed.

> *Enter—Right Front—*MILLY, *carrying a tray*
> *containing a reddish-colored liquid in*
> *glasses. She stops before* BLAVER.

BLAVER (*to* MILLY).
Ah,—what is this?
MILLY.   Iced tea.
BLAVER.   Why, that will be
Refreshing, very!

> (*To* MISS P.)
> Here!
> (*Pointing to chairs surrounding a small table,*
> *near the bay window, and motioning her to*
> *sit down*).
>   Iced tea!
> (*To* MILLY.)
>   Yes, yes.
> (BLAVER *and* MISS P. *sit at the table.* MILLY
> *places two glasses of the reddish-colored*
> *liquid before them.*)

BLAVER (*continuing the interrupted conversation*).
Where there's no levity, affairs like this
Create it. I've known sober-minded men
Grow indiscreet—

> (*tasting the tea.*)
>   This is good, yes—and make
All their professions seem ridiculous.

Enter—Left and Right—couples walking together.
*Exit—Left Upper—*Milly.
*Enter—Right Upper—*Jem *carrying a tray on which*
are plates containing refreshments to eat.
Miss Primwood (*looking in disapprobation at the*
couples).
And scenes like this, too, tend to cause flirtation—
(*looking at two elderly people together.*)
In those so old, too, they should be above it.
(Miss Primwood's *spoon that she has been*
*using, falls to the floor.—*Blaver *hands*
Miss P. *his spoon that he has not used, at*
the same time picking up Miss P's. *spoon*
and significantly placing it in his own cup.)
Blaver. Precisely!
Miss P. Yes, at times, it makes me feel——
Blaver (*who evidently has lost the connection of*
thought).
Flirtation makes you feel?
Miss P. (*in evident disgust*).
Oh no; not that!
(Jem *stands before them with his tray.*)
Blaver (*noticing* Jem, *and taking plates from his tray*
for Miss P. *and himself, as if thinking* Miss
P. *referred to these*).
Oh yes, I see!
Miss P. (*disliking his inference with reference to the*
meaning of her former words).
No, no!

Blaver (*referring to the plates*).

　　　　　　　　　　　　　　Not take them?

Miss P.　　　　　　　　　　　　　　　　These?

　　Oh yes, I thank you.—You mistook my meaning.

　　I do not think one ought to feel at all.

Blaver.　No, in flirtation none should feel at all.

Miss P.　No, no, no! not in that—in anything.

　　If none would feel, none would have discontent;

　　And that would cure all evils of the time.

Blaver.　Yes, that is so.　Why, even small boys

　　　　now,

　　Must have small beer——

Miss P.　　　　　　　Something to pop, you know!

　　The key-note of our age is discontent.

　　Our slaves now even hint of earning wages;

　　And girls, once clad in bonnets and in slippers,

　　Now strut in hats and boots.

Blaver.　　　　　　　　　And where, strut where?

Miss P.　Ah, that's well put, my friend.　They

　　　　strut to schools

　　In which they study, think and talk like boys.

Blaver.　And times that do not like a cackling

　　　　hen,

　　And seek to fill their coops with fowl that crow,

　　Will not get many eggs.

Miss P.　　　　　　　　No, no; no, no!—

　　Think what a scandal, if our highest courts——

Blaver.　Should not court women of the highest

　　　　kind.

Miss P.   Precisely; and o'errule th' iniquity
That gives free entrance into men's resorts
Of maids——

Blaver.   That in your school are prized like jewels!

(Blaver *and* Miss P. *continue their conversation
aside.*)

Enter—Left Upper—Cecil *and* Father Hycher
talking earnestly.

Cecil.   Yes, Father Hycher ; but you know our laws
Have never recognized the churches thus.

Father H.   But we have rights—

Cecil.   To change the laws you have,
But not to break them.

Father H.   Did one merely waive
The letter of the law, what could be harmed ?

Cecil.   One's conscience, if he went against the law.
'Twould not be right,—a fact, I take it, Father,
You ought to see.

Father H.   I do not see it so ;
And if I did, above it I could see
A higher law.

*Exit—Left Second—*Father H.

Cecil   (*looking after him, and soliloquizing*).
                         Humph, humph ! we live to learn.
It seems that even formalists like him
Can see some spirit through a form ; but what ?—
One time upon a mountain top, I saw
My own shape magnified on clouds about me.
How many more in earth's high places find,

Looming on clouds of false regard about them,
False forms of self, distorted in their size !
To waken such to their own true position,
Thank heaven for precipices !   When they fall,
Their views of God and self, turned upside down,
May bring, at last, conversion.

(CECIL *moves toward the right near where* BLAVER
        and MISS P. *are sitting.   Both rise.*)

MISS P.   Oh, Professor,
Professor Cecil, how your ears must burn !
We've heard the rumors that are in the wind.

CECIL   (*bowing and motioning them to be seated*).
Trust not to words with only wind to back them.
There's nothing quite so empty as the sky
Behind a blow, when once it has blown by.

(*All sit,* CECIL *taking a vacant chair at the table.*)

MISS P.   That's well for you to say ; but you two
        friends,

                (*bowing to* BLAVER.)

Your judgment,

                (*bowing to* CECIL.)

                and your judgments, when they rule
Our civil, social, educational ways,
Will put an end to some things.

CECIL.   ⸳ To their life ?

MISS P.   How you enjoy a joke !—You've read,
        not so ?

                (*gesturing toward* BLAVER.)

The deacon's latest work ?

CECIL. To tell the truth,
I've not had time.
MISS P. So, little interest !—
CECIL. Of course the question has two sides——
BLAVER (*aside*).

Two sides ?—
It has but one. I see that he's not with us.
MISS P. The great book of the age !
BLAVER (*to* MISS P).

You flatter me.
(*to* CECIL).
She likes my essay, since, on general grounds,
As I detail the duties of the state,
I argue prohibition by the whole
Of all things detrimental to the part,
Applying this, not only to the cause
To which my life is pledged, but with this, too,
To questions like the giving of instruction
To slaves, and free tuition to poor whites,
And throwing open to our girls and women
The State schools, not designed to train their sex.
'Tis my discussion of this latter point
Enlists her praise, whose long—
(MISS P. *straightens up and draw back.*)
no, I mean wide—
Whose wide experience, as the principal
Of our first female college, seals her right
To criticise all efforts of the State
To train our girls in different schools from hers.

CECIL (*in good-natured banter*).
   Ah, yes, I see.   The same boat floats you both.
   You   pull   together.   Friends   are   worth   the
      having
   Who best can serve themselves when serving us.
MISS P.   Oh, you must read his book !   You'll like
      it too ;
   If but for what it says of slaves and women.
CECIL.   You class the two together ?   I should not.
                    (*aside.*)
   How women love their fetters !—But 'tis well.
   They make sweet slaves, but very bitter masters.
MISS P.   You would not open then our college doors
   To women ?
CECIL.   Why not ?
MISS P.   Why, our boys and girls
   Might fall in love !
CECIL.   That would be no new thing ;
   And, being wont to walk in love, when young,
   They might be much less prone to fall in love,
   In ways not wise, when older.
MISS P.   But their minds
   Are so unlike !—
CECIL.   And never can be matched
   Until they learn to share each other's aims.
   Souls are not mated when two forms of flesh
   Join hands, or merely share each other's arms.
MISS P. And   you   would   have   them   like   each
      other?

CECIL.   Yes.

'Tis quite important if they are to marry.

Like ought to go with like. And paths that
    push

Young men and maids together, whet their wits

And make their weddings wise ones.

MISS P.   Always ?

CECIL.   No ;

But oftener, yes much oftener so, than elsewise.

Where true love is the treasure to be sought.

One glimpse of nature is a better guide

Than all the forms of calculating art

That ever powdered an instinctive flush,

Or rouged pale hate, in any masquerade

That men call good society.

MISS P.   One scarce

Would think you had so much romance in you.

CECIL.   All have romance, if only they have soul.

'Tis in the expression of it that they differ.

*Enter—Left Upper—*JEM *with tray holding more
    refreshments.*

MISS P.   And most of them believe, with Deacon
    Blaver,

It should not be expressed in schools.

CECIL.   Why not ?

Romance is but that region of the soul

Whose sun is love, within which, when we dwell,

Each act of duty and each thought of truth

Is haloed with a light that seems like heaven's.

To spirits rightly moved, the whole of life,—
Home, school, religion,—ought to hoard romance.
        (JEM *speaks aside to* CECIL.)
CECIL (*rising*).
(BLAVER *and* MISS P. *rise while* CECIL *gestures
   toward chairs,* JEM *and the refreshments.*)
  Oh, pray be seated, and take more.
MISS P.   Thanks.
BLAVER.   Thanks.
(JEM *removes from table the empty glasses and plates,
   and substitutes full ones.*)
MISS P. And do you then approve, do you admire
  These short-haired women, and these long-haired
    men,
  Exchanging shawls and coats, and stripping life
  Of character, to make it caricature?
      *Exit—Left Upper Entrance—*JEM.
CECIL. I do not much admire the straw in spring
  That forms the spread of flower-beds; but
    beneath
  Sleep summer's fairest offspring. What you moot
  May show two sides. I've seen a man run
    down
  Amid the clash and clangor of a street,
  Because one ear was deaf. In any sphere,
  The rush of life may run down all who hear
  But on one side.
     *Enter—Right Upper Entrance—*FREEMAN.
MISS P.   But when one side is right.

CECIL. The right is that to which the world moves
on.

You cross its track to stop it ; it moves on,
You fall.

(CECIL *bows and turns toward* FREEMAN. BLAVER
and MISS P. *bow, then reseat themselves.*)

MISS P. And this he does not mean to do
For my cause or for yours. Trust me for that.

BLAVER. His friends must see he does not get so
high

That falling far will hurt him.

(BLAVER *and* MISS P. *continue to eat and drink,
and talk aside, till, after a little,* BLAVER
*points vigorously toward the Right Second
Entrance. Then both rise, taking plates
and glasses with them, and exeunt at
Right Second Entrance.*)

*Enter—Left Upper Entrance—*MADAM CECIL,
MADAM LOWE *and* LOWE, *carrying his
plans, also* JEM.

MADAM CECIL (*to* JEM).

Here, you say ?—

(*To* CECIL.)

Oh, here you are ! Come look at these —

(*Pointing to* LOWE'S *plans.*)

these plans,

They're just the thing the city needs. And we've
Been searching all the house for you.

*Exit—Right Upper Entrance—*JEM.

(Madam Cecil *and* Madam Lowe *remain near Left
Upper Entrance.*)

Cecil *motions to* Freeman *indicating that he
look at the plans with him, which* Freeman *does.*

Cecil (*replying partly to* Madam C. *and partly speaking to* Lowe).

                                  I see.

Lowe (*pointing to a part of the plan*). And see the
church here?

Cecil.   Oh! is that the church?
But I thought you a friend?

Lowe.   The company
Are world's folk—will not build a meeting. So
We would not quarrel with them. We build this.

Freeman (*laughing good-naturedly*).
You beat the Masonic order. They but make
A show of their religion when they lay
A corner-stone. You lay out for it now.

Lowe. Ah yes! With me religion is the chief
Consideration. Think how poor our life
Would be without religion.

Freeman.   Be less rich,
You think.

Lowe.   Just so; and so there's nothing like
A church to elevate the character——

Freeman. Of real estate, I see.

Lowe (*half realizing that he is being made a butt*).
                   No, we don't mean——

FREEMAN. No people live here yet?

LOWE.   Ah, but they will——

FREEMAN. If you do what 'tis right to do for them.
To build a church is right—not so?—and right
Is your religion.

LOWE.   Yes ; but one might think
His motives were not rightly understood.

FREEMAN (*glancing toward* CECIL *significantly*).
I think we understand them perfectly.

LOWE (*looking particularly toward* CECIL).
And like the plans then ?

FREEMAN.   Oh, he must—as plans.
They plan so far ahead.

LOWE.   Ah, if one see
A mountain in his path that must be climbed,
He'll make more effort.   Effort's what we need.
With such a plan as this, our friends will know
We need more money, and will find us more.

CECIL. That's true.

(MADAM CECIL *comes to them*. FREEMAN *turns to
speak to* MADAM LOWE.)

LOWE (*to* CECIL).
             · Am glad to meet such approbation.

CECIL. Not that exactly ! Wise men ride no
hobby
Before a cool mood tests its hoofs—should have
To study this.

Exeunt — Right Upper Entrance—FREEMAN *and*
MADAM LOWE.

Lowe (*half in earnest turning to* Madam Cecil.).
　　　　　　If friends must judge like foes,
What good then does it do to have a friend?
Cecil (*earnestly and good-naturedly*).
　To prove to all the justice of our souls
　That wish for friends both generous and just.—
　　　(*Taking the plans in his hands.*)
　'Tis difficult to take these in, at first.
　　　*Enter—Right Upper Entrance—*Jem.
Madam C. (*to* Lowe, *as if with a covert meaning*).
　You leave them here, and we'll look over them.
　　　(*She motions toward* Jem, *to whom* Cecil
　　　　*hands the plans, at the same time motion-
　　　　ing to him to take them to the Left.* Jem
　　　　turns, and presently,)
　　　*Exit—Left Second Entrance—*Jem.
(*When* Cecil *and* Madam C. *turn toward* Jem, Lowe
　turns toward the Right Third Entrance.)
Lowe (*to* Himself),
　And when the time comes that he needs a friend,
　I'll take him in too and look over him.
　　　*Exit—Right Third Entrance—*Lowe.
Madam C. (*to* Cecil, *and evidently annoyed to see*
　　　Lowe *leaving them*).
　Kraft, Hycher, Lowe and Blaver,—all, to-night,
　All frown at things that you have said to them.
　Why will you always give these men offense?
Cecil.　Because I give them truth.

MADAM C.   Truth is for fools.

CECIL.   I give it to them.

MADAM C.   Humph ! It comes from fools.

CECIL.   Yes, if they think men want it. I do not.
   They only need it.

MADAM C.   Need ? What for ?

CECIL.   Their good—
   Their own, and—say—humanity's.

MADAM C.   The good
   All seek from men like you, is leadership.
   But he who leads men up, himself must mount,
   Where he is seen above them.

CECIL.   How and where
   He mounts, depends on that in which he leads.
   A leader in the truth had better kneel
   Upon the footstool of a throne, than sit
   Upon it, crowned by falsehood.

MADAM C.   Would you were,
   But what I thought you were when we were wed !

CECIL (*kindly*).
   Come, come, your wishes, like wild steeds, escape
   The reining of your reason, and may wreck it.
   Why wish a station higher than we have ?

MADAM C.   For you—your influence.

CECIL.   Nay, in that you err.
   True words alone are weapons of true thought.
   If I be free to use these, I am free
   To be truth's champion. If, to gain the place

You wish me, or to hold it, being gained,
I let my tongue be tied, I'm but a slave.
MADAM C.
    A woman wrecked at sea, had better lash
The anchor to her throat, than try to breast
The waves of life in such a world as this,
Wed to a man without ambition.   She
Could not sink sooner.
CECIL (*gazing and gesturing at their surroundings*).
                     Do you sink, my wife,
With these surroundings ?
MADAM C.   Yes, for power and wealth
Both loom before you.   When I tell it you,
And strive to urge you toward them, you, blind
    loot,
Squat, blinking like an owl ; or, if you stir,
But flutter, blunder, miss your aim, and fall
From off the very branch, the topmost branch,
You ought to perch upon.
CECIL.   Alas, my wife,
I thought you loved me for the man I was.
I never wrought nor wished for wealth.
MADAM C.   Oh, drone,
That I could sting you, as do bees their drones
That make no honey !
CECIL.   You do sting at times.
This ought to please you. But you've better
    moods.
I never could have thought I loved you else.

Why blame my soul, because it must be true
To higher aims and higher influence ?
If, seeking these, this world's promotion come,
Let come ! I'll take it then by right divine.

MADAM C. Fanatic ! Do you think in men's mad
rush,
Each towards his own life's goal, they wrest the
power
That makes another serve them, without work ?—
Skill ? shrewdness ? tact? and forcing to the wall,
Or down the precipice, each weaker rival ?

CECIL. I do, if power that crowns them come from
God.

MADAM C. The power that crowns one with success
on earth
Is earthly. Keen men know this. 'Tis not God :
The devil rules the world.

CECIL. God overrules it.

MADAM C. In far results, but in the near ones
never !

CECIL. Then look to far results. Transferring
there
These transient whims of yours, you'll find them
melt,
Like summer mist, while, rock-bound under them,
Each goal remains that your true nature craves.
Why seek for riches, when we have enough ?

MADAM C. Enough ! Oh, sluggard ! Have **we**
that ?

4

CECIL.   We have—
Enough for comfort, not enough for care ;
Enough to make us grateful for the wage
Rewarding earnest work ; but not enough
To bind long habit to the fate of those
Whose serving earth has made them slaves to it.
The peace of life crowns competence, not wealth.
The wise man wants no more.

MADAM C.   But woman does.

*Exit—Left Second Entrance—*MADAM CECIL.

CECIL. Then let no wise man marry. Cursed
      fate !—
This striving to walk on in paths of right,
And knowing every pace takes one more stride
Away from all one loves !—From all one loves ?—
No, no ;—from all that, once, one thought he loved.
Oh, cruel customs of a cruel world,
Which damn us for those dreams that seem to be
Our holiest inspirations !   Cruel dreams,
That never prove delusions, till the world
Welds bonds for us that death alone can break !
And cruel bonds that make all happiness,
In one so bound, impossibility,
Unless he sell his soul, or—who is this ?

*Enter—Right Second Entrance—*CELIA.

Why, Celia !

CELIA.   I have come to tell you, friend,
The man I fear is here.   I saw his face,
And like a thunder-cloud foretelling storm——

CECIL. We'll go first where we'll not be overheard.

*Exeunt—Left Upper Entrance—*CECIL *and* CELIA.

*Enter—Right Upper Entrance—*FREEMAN *and* FAITH.

FREEMAN. You love me, Faith. Your manner tells
 me so.

FAITH. Your rival, Freeman, is no man, mere man.

FREEMAN. You are deceived. You vow through—
 to—a man.

 Who'll use you—God knows how! the door is
 locked :

He holds the key. Your uncle, though a priest,
Has eyes upon your wealth. The thing is proved.
Your dying father feared this. Faith, I know
His wish for you. Trust him, trust me, your
 friend,
Disrobed of mystery, save th' eternal one
Which thrills us now, whom heaven has made for
 mates.

FAITH. I would not give you up, except to wed
A holier spouse.

FREEMAN.   Yet one that is, at times,
A Moloch, clasping in his arms of fire
Desires he kindles, but can never quench.

FAITH. Oh, Freeman, when you speak, I tremble so !
You fill my soul with fears for you ; but, oh,
With fears that are so sweet, again I fear
That my own soul is what I should fear most.

FREEMAN. Let's fright away our fears by facing
 them.

Will you not be my bride? Be this and use
Your freedom as your father would have wished.
*Enter—Left Second Entrance—*FATHER HYCHER.
FATHER H. (*to* FAITH).

What?—Have I warned you, Faith, so many
times?
And you still parley with this infidel?—
Obey me now!—Away, no more of this!

> (FAITH *moves toward Left Upper Entrance—*
> FREEMAN *starts to follow her.* FATHER
> HYCHER *calls to him.*)

You will not follow her?—

*Exit—Left Upper Entrance—*FAITH.

FREEMAN. No?—wherefore not?
FATHER H. I am her uncle.
FREEMAN. Not her father, though!
FATHER H. Her spirit's—I direct her steps.
FREEMAN. Step-father?—

In that rôle men like you are just ideal!
But I am, that which you are not—her friend.

FATHER H. You are a young man with a young
man's dreams.

FREEMAN. You are an old man with an old man's
schemes.
And she has wealth, and you have use for it.

FATHER H. And you think you have none! Oho,
young man,
When you have read yourself, you may be heard
When trying to read others. But we waste

Our time. I am her guardian; and you
Should act the gentleman.

FREEMAN.   Which when I act,
I'll not take lessons in the art from you.

FATHER H.   Take this at least.—A gentleman is one
Who never does the unexpected.

FREEMAN.   Well,
    By that test you can pass. I grant it you.
    All you have done has been in character.
    You call me infidel; but, Father Hycher,
    The infidel is one who does not trust
    The power that made and moves the soul within.
    If Faith did not desire another life
    Than you have planned, you might be wise and
       kind.

FATHER H.   Poor youth, when you know more
      about the world——

FREEMAN.   I shall know more about such men as
      you ;
    Know how the dust of earth can make one blind,
    And din can make one deaf, till skies can blaze
    And heaven's voice thunder, yet no sight nor
      sound
    Reach——

FATHER H.   (*sarcastically.*)
                What ?—

FREEMAN.   What was a soul ! But there are souls
    Are stolen when they're stoled. The devil's hand
    Out-does the deacon's, and there's nothing left

But vestment.   All the barterer's priceless birth-
    right
Goes for the mess of pottage that he feeds on.
Not strange such like to limit others' joys,
Turn nature inside out and upside down,
Claim spirit rules where all are slaves of sense,
And heaven their crown whose schemes are rimmed
    by hell.

FATHER H.   Humph, humph, young man !   You'll
    yet repent of this.

*Exit—Left Second Entrance—*FATHER HYCHER.

*Enter—Left Upper Entrance—*CECIL *and* CELIA.

CECIL   (*to* FREEMAN.)

Why, friend, you seem excited.   What has roiled
    you ?

FREEMAN.   Oh nothing,   nothing,   nothing but a
    toad   ꞏ
That squat upon a flower here in your garden !

CECIL.   Here is a flower that you may save from
    this.
I must attend the guests, and this, our friend,
Needs your protection.   She will tell you why.
I leave her with you.

*Enter—Left Upper Entrance—*MADAM CECIL.

    (CECIL *continues to* CELIA, *taking her hand.*)
               And remember, Celia,
You must not fail to stay with us to-night.

MADAM CECIL (*aside*).

I thought so !   I have spied this play before.

Men seldom waive the wishes of their wives
Except to welcome other women's wishes.
Kraft and myself will scotch this pretty game.
(*to* CECIL, *while* CELIA *talks aside to* FREEMAN, *after
both have bowed to* CECIL.)
You had forgotten you had other guests.
A storm is coming on.   They start to leave ;
And we must speed their parting.   Shall we go ?
(CECIL *and* MADAM C. *move toward the Left
Second Entrance*—FREEMAN *and* CELIA
*move toward the bay window at the
Right.*)
FREEMAN (*motioning toward the bay window*).
Let's stay in here, and we'll be out the way.
Exeunt—Left Second Entrance—CECIL *and*
MADAM C.   FREEMAN *and* CECIL *seat
themselves in the bay window.*
Enter—Left Upper—FATHER *and* WIDOW HYCHER.
FATHER HYCHER (*to* WIDOW HYCHER).
Let him have all her money that you live on ?—
Not I !
WIDOW H. (*to* FATHER H).   He shall not call on
Faith again.
FATHER H.   You'll say she's out?
WIDOW H.   I will.—And you, you liked
The stole ?
FATHER H.   One could not be embroidered better.
With just the shade——
WIDOW H.   For your complexion, yes.

FATHER H.   Your candlesticks too go so well now
  with——
FREEMAN (*to* CELIA).
  The fiddlesticks?
FATHER H. (*to* WIDOW H.).
                                    The other ornaments.
WIDOW H. (*to* FATHER H.).
  They're always just before you when you pray?
FATHER H. (*to* WIDOW H.).
  And make me think of you.
WIDOW H. (*to* FATHER H.).
                                    And make heaven too?——
  No matter what one does?
FATHER H. (*to* Widow H.).
                                    Who could forget
  Your deeds in rendering the church attractive?
FREEMAN (*to* CELIA).
  Especially in the front pew with her bonnet,—
  So sweet!—a hanging garden!
FATHER H. (*to* WIDOW H.).
                                    All note this.
FREEMAN (*to* CELIA).
  The very bees can't help but buzz about it.
WIDOW H. (*to* FATHER H.).
  And Cecil—will he aid you?
FATHER H. (*to* WIDOW H.).
                                    Humph! a cause
  That's lost is not the one I follow.
*Exeunt—Left Second—*FATHER HYCHER *and* WIDOW
                    HYCHER.

CECIL (*to* FREEMAN). Cause ?—
Does he mean Cecil's ?
FREEMAN. Hope so ! Happy Cecil !—
'Twill be high noon for him when he can see
A form like that one shadowing him no more.
CELIA. I think it always seems high noon to those
Who trample all their shadows underfoot
As he does.
*Enter—Right Upper Entrance—*LOWE *and* MADAM
LOWE.
(*The stage becomes gradually darker.*)
FREEMAN (*pointing toward Right Upper Entrance*).
Yes, that's true. But what of those
Who deem it wise to keep themselves in shade,
Held as a shield to ward away the light
With every ray of color that might reach them,
As if they feared 'twas their worst enemy ?
LOWE (*to* MADAM LOWE).
The air seems weighted with a coming storm.
FREEMAN (*to* CELIA).
Their air appears so. Yes.
MADAM L. (*to* LOWE).
Must hurry home.
(*Thunder in the distance*)
How near ! We should have been at meeting !
LOWE (*to* MADAM L.
Yes,
But if we had been there, how could one then
Have shown those plans ?

MADAM L. (*to* LOWE).
                    Of course, we had to come,
But this man Cecil's not religious.
LOWE (*to* MADAM L.).
                    No ;
You heard how they made light of that new build-
    ing,—
And for their own sect too !
MADAM L. (*to* LOWE).
                    Yes, I have heard
Enough for once.   That irreligious music !
LOWE (*to* MADAM L.).
And noise and dancing !   Well, 'twas fortunate
That our refreshments came so early.
MADAM L. (*to* LOWE).   Yes.

(*Distant thunder.*)

LOWE (*to* MADAM L.).
There's one good thing : this thunder storm will
    end it.
*Exeunt—Left Upper Entrance—*LOWE *and* MADAM
                    LOWE.
FREEMAN (*to* CELIA).
I wonder if they really grudge each draft
Of those enjoying what is past their taste?
'Tis sad to think it, yet one sometimes must,
That there's no conscience goads like conscious
    envy ;
None seem so zealous as when they are jealous.

(*Thunder louder than before.* Celia *and* Freeman
both rise.)
But hear the storm,   I think 'tis best you stay
In Cecil's study.
(Freeman *points toward Left Second Entrance.*)
Celia (*pointing toward the right*).
                    We can pass through here.
Freeman.   I'll go at once, and call two men I
    know,
Detectives—good ones—they will shadow him.
Exeunt — Right   Front   Entrance — Freeman *and*

Celia.

*Enter—Left Upper Entrance—*Blaver, Lowe,
    Miss Primwood *and* Madam Lowe, *and
    others, all with hats and cloaks, evidently
    prepared to leave the house.*

Blaver (*to* Lowe).
I used to have some confidence in Cecil.
Lowe (*to* Blaver).
But now he shows such lack of enterprise!
Blaver.   'Tis clear to me, he'll never aid my plans,
Nor yours.
*Enter—Left Upper Entrance—*Madam Cecil, *fol-
    lowed by* Jem.
Lowe.   And wise men, when they fear a fight,
Will never lend one weapon to a foe.
Madam C. (*to* Miss Primwood).
You leave us in a storm.

BLAVER (*to* MADAM CECIL).

              It will clear off.

MADAM C. And when the sun is shining here, you
    know

Where you can find a friend.

BLAVER (*rather significantly, as he offers his arm to*
    MISS PRIMWOOD).

                    Yes—one—I do.

I thank you for a very pleasant evening.

        (*Shaking hands with* MADAM C.)

MADAM C. (*shaking hands with* BLAVER).

Good evening.

             (*To* JEM.)

        Here, Jem, show them to the gate.

    MADAM C. *motions to* JEM *who moves toward*
        Right Upper Entrance—MISS PRIMWOOD,
        then LOWE, *then* MADAM LOWE, *also*
        others, shake hands with MADAM C.

MISS P. Good-night.

MADAM C.   Good-night.

LOWE.   Good-night.

MADAM L.   Good-night.

MADAM C.   Good-night.

    Exeunt—Right Upper Entrance—BLAVER *with*
        MISS PRIMWOOD, LOWE *with* MADAM
        LOWE *and others.*

    Enter—Right Third Entrance—KRAFT.

MADAM C. (*to* KRAFT).

Have all our guests gone?

(*Thunder and storm increase.*)

KRAFT.   No ; for I am here.

MADAM C.   You feel at home without the going
   there ?

KRAFT.   And where's your husband ?

MADAM C.   With some guests, perhaps.

KRAFT.   Or, say, with Celia.

MADAM C.   What ?—Your scheme
   has failed ?

KRAFT.   Not yet ; my men are here.

*Enter—Right Upper Entrance—*JEM.

(*Thunder and lightning—*KRAFT *points toward* JEM.)
                                 You send for him,
   I'll send my men for her.

*Exit—Right Third Entrance—*KRAFT.

MADAM C. (*to* JEM).
                        Jem, find your master.
   I wish to see him.   Tell him 'tis important.

*Exit—Right Upper Entrance—*JEM.
(*to herself.*)

Now let him leave her but one little moment,
As leave he must, and they will have her seized.
And may a pall, as black as tops this night,
           (*Thunder and lightning*).
Come down, and hide her face from him forever.
Oh, naught but death, or burial deep as death,
Can ever fitly robe a form once wedged
Between a man and wife !—Though what care I ?—

Kraft hates my husband ; yet is wholly mine ;
And so I get my wish.
                    (*Thunder and lightning.*)
            *Enter—Right Upper Entrance—*CECIL.
CECIL (*to* MADAM CECIL).   What is your wish ?
MADAM C.   And what care you, my husband, for
    my wish ?
Oh, I was but a fool, to wed a fool !
Like goes with like.   I now acknowledge it.
                    (*Thunder and lightning.*)
You might have been—ah me !—what might you
    not ?
Position, wealth,—all waited on your nod.
You have dismissed them by your course to-night ;
But one hope now remains, and that through
    Kraft.
Enter—Right First Entrance—in trepidation, CELIA.
                    (*Thunder and lightning.*)
CELIA.   Help ! help !
CECIL (*to* CELIA).

                    I'm here.   What is it ?
CELIA.   Kraft with men !
    They come to take me.
CECIL.   That they shall not do.
MADAM C.   Wait !   'Tis her guardian claims her.
    Who are you ?
CECIL.   A man who shields a woman.
MADAM C.   If she lie ?—
CECIL.   He's free to prove it.

MADAM C.   Dare you tell him that?—
Him, Kraft,—the man on whom alone depends
Your chance now for promotion?
> (*Thunder and lightning.*)

CELIA (*to* CECIL.)
                    Do not harm
Yourself.

CECIL (*to* CELIA).
                    But sacrifice this gentle lamb
To wild ambition?—Never!—Hide in here!
> (CECIL *points toward Left Upper Entrance.*)
> *Exit—Left Upper Entrance*—CELIA.

MADAM C. (*to* CECIL).
You do not know—They claim her as a slave.

CECIL (*to* MADAM C.). I save her as a woman.

MADAM C.   But the law—
The sentiment—the spirit of the State.—
You dare not shield her.
> (*Thunder and lightning.*)

CECIL.   Wherefore dare I not?

MADAM C. No man has ever yet with us been
    left
Not ruined—left to live, who ventured this.
Your influence, your position, property,
Your life, my home, my hope for you,—all, all
Would all be forfeited.
> (*Thunder and lightning.*)

CECIL.   Well, let them go.

When they have stripped me of all things be-
　　sides,
I'll have a clean, clear conscience, death and
　　heaven.

MADAM C.　You are a madman.

CECIL.　　　　　　　　　　　　Not so mad as you :
　I wait for proof.

MADAM C.　　　　　And if they prove their case ?—

CECIL.　They'll wait then till they take her.　But
　they come.
　　　　　　　　(*Thunder and lightning.*)

*Enter—Right Front Entrance—*KRAFT *with two men.*

KRAFT (*to* CECIL).
　Is Celia here ?
　　　(*advancing toward Left Upper Entrance.*)
　　　　　　　　　I say, is Celia here ?

CECIL (*standing in front of Left Upper Entrance—
　　and looking around*).
　I do not see her here.

KRAFT.　　　　　　　I too have eyes.
　I did not ask you that.　She's in this house.

CECIL.　She was my guest ; if she be still within
　Then she is still my guest.

KRAFT.　　　　　　　I am her guardian.

CECIL.　And so am I, while I remain her host.
　　　　　(*Thunder and lightning.*)
　　　(CECIL *looks at the men behind* KRAFT.)
You seem to wish to guard her well,—too well.

KRAFT. I'm more than guardian. She belongs to
me.

CECIL. Well, prove your case.

KRAFT. You ask for proof from me,—
A gentleman?—

CECIL. I ask for proof from you.

KRAFT. You hint I am no gentleman?

CECIL. I say
You are not gentle in your present mood ;
And that child is—too gentle far for you.

KRAFT. What?—You defy me?—I shall search for
her.
(*Thunder and lightning.*)

CECIL. Not till you get by me !
(CECIL *pulls out a pistol.* MADAM C. *seizes it.*)

KRAFT. And that we shall !
(KRAFT *dashes at* CECIL, *followed by his men.
Pistol fired behind scene, but apparently on
stage.* CECIL *falls. Terrific thunder
and lightning.*)

*Enter—Right Upper Entrance—*FREEMAN *with two
detectives.*

FREEMAN. Here! seize them ! Stop the villains,
every one !

*Exeunt—Left Second Entrance—*KRAFT *and men,
followed by detectives.*

*Enter—Left Upper Entrance—*CELIA, *and
bends over* CECIL, *excitedly examining into
his condition.*

5

(FREEMAN *snatches pistol from* MADAM C., *saying to her,*)

Aha, you are the murderer ? you ? eh ?—you ?

MADAM C.   I did not fire it.

FREEMAN (*examining pistol*).

One ball gone !   Who did ?—
Confess it, or convict your lover, Kraft.

CELIA (*wringing hands over* CECIL'S *prostrate body*).
Oh, he is dead for me !—The only man
I ever loved is 'dead for me, for me !

(*Thunder and lightning.*)

CURTAIN.

ACT SECOND.

SCENE FIRST : *A sick chamber. At the Left, between the Front and Second Entrances, is an alcove; in this, visible to the audience, is a bed, beside the bed is a chair and a small table, and on the latter are bottles and glasses. On the bed,* CECIL *lies insensible, with his head to the audience and his face toward the stage. Just behind* CECIL, *lying also on the bed, but concealed in this scene, is an effigy exactly resembling him. Forming the back curtain of the stage, is a wall containing a bell-cord, windows, possibly a door, etc.*

ENTRANCES : *by doors at the Right and Left Front and Second, the Left Second Entrance leading apparently to the space behind the bed in the alcove.*

The curtain rising discloses a PHYSICIAN *sitting in the chair beside the bed, and* CELIA *just entering the room, or standing near him.*

CELIA (*aside*).
How fortunate for Freeman and myself
That Kraft and Madam Cecil should have fled

And left to us the man they thought was mur-
    dered !
Now we can nurse him, as he should be nursed.
                    (*to the* PHYSICIAN.)
How does he seem this morning ?
PHYSICIAN.   Very low.
CELIA.   You fear he never will recover, then ?
PHYSICIAN (*rising from chair, and offering it to*
    CELIA).
    'Tis hard to tell—no other case just like it.
    One would not think a bullet lodged where this is
    Enough to insulate the brain entirely,
    Yet not a nerve will act.   He scarcely seems
    To see, or hear, or even feel one touch him.
CELIA (*looking at* CECIL).
    'Tis just like death.
PHYSICIAN.   Yes, very much like death.
CELIA.   He seems to think, though.
PHYSICIAN.   Certainly.   He's living.
CELIA.   In states like this, what can a person think
    of ?
PHYSICIAN.   Why, he must dream of what he did,
    and was,
    And wished to be, before he reached them.
CELIA.   So ?
PHYSICIAN.   Of course, there's nothing else for him
    to think of.
CELIA.   I've sometimes thought he knows that I
    am by.

PHYSICIAN (*rising and preparing to leave*).
    Perhaps he does. At any sign of it,
    Attempt to make him conscious of your presence,
    And keep him so. 'Tis said that things as slight
    As flickering flames, attracting consciousness
    At times, if they but set the nerves to thrilling,
    Wake slumbering senses into life again.
CELIA. I will. You'll come to-morrow, will you
    not?
PHYSICIAN. Oh, certainly! Good-day.
CELIA (*accompanying the* PHYSICIAN *to the Right
    Second entrance*).

                      Good-day.

        *Exit—Right Second—*PHYSICIAN.

CELIA *looks back toward* CECIL *and crosses to alcove*).

                    Poor man!
    Can this be Cecil?—Cecil had a soul.—
    And where now has it flown?—I wonder if
    My voice could ever really call him back!
    I'll try it. I will sit here day by day,
    And take his hand in mine, as I would lead
    His body, were he in the body still;
    And though he may not hear the thing I say,
    Nor even feel me touch him, who can tell
    But I may find his spirit in its dreams,
    And comfort him, and draw him here once more.
(*She apparently passes around the foot of the bed to its
    other side.*)
        *Exit—Left Second—*CELIA.

SCENE SECOND : *The stage is darkened, and the curtain forming the back of the room in Scene First rises, leaving everything on the stage the same as in this scene with exception of that which is back of the Right and Left Second Entrances. At the rear of the stage, is an extensive sylvan landscape, trees, rocks, mosses, etc., backed by higher rocks and distant mountain scenery. The leaves are colored as in autumn, and the sky as at sunrise. Golden light illumines the stage. Backing, near the center of the stage, slightly elevated and containing seats overlooking the stage, is an arbor. Some of the stone or moss-covered steps leading up to this can be used as seats. Around and behind the arbor are other steps leading upward. Entrances, used in this scene : Right and Left Third and Upper ; and Back Center, behind the arbor, and reached by passing upward either through it or around it.*

From the moment that the stage is darkened, and while it is gradually being illumined again, the following is chanted by a choir, either invisible to the audience, or, clothed in white, and arranged at the rear of the stage :

Oh, who has known the whole of light,
   That knows it day by day,
Where suns that make the morning bright,
   At evening, pass away ?

Before the day, beyond the day,
  Above the suns that roll,
There was a light, there waits a light
  That never leaves the soul.

Oh, who has weighed the worth of light,
  That gauged it by the gleam
That came within the range of sight
  And thought the rest a dream?
Before that sight, beyond that sight
  And all that mortals deem,
There was a light, there waits a light,
  Where things are all they seem.

Once or twice toward the close of the singing,
Cecil sits up in the bed in a bewildered
way, passing his hand over his forehead.
As the last strains die away, he stands
on the floor, leaving an exact effigy of him-
self lying on the bed behind him. He now
appears clothed in white with knee breeches.
As he begins to gaze wonderingly about
him,
Enter—Left Third Entrance—Cecilia, an
idealized form of Celia, clothed also in
white, Grecian style. Cecil does not
see her till after she has spoken.

Cecil. Ah, where am I?
Cecilia.   With me.
Cecil (*looking at her in astonishment, yet shrinking*
from her as if in awe).
                      And who are you?

CECILIA.   Your friend.

CECIL   (*drawing nearer her*).

My friend?

CECILIA.   Do I seem else?

CECIL   (*with pleased bewilderment*).

Nay, nay

You seem it all: you seem far more than this;
Yet where—when—was it, that I knew you so?

CECILIA.   You knew me so?—You think you knew
me, then?

CECIL.   Yes, knew you; and I know you; yet seem
not
To know where, when or how I learned of you.

> (CECIL *gazes around, then looking back at the
> bed that he has left, he suddenly starts upon
> seeing there the effigy of himself.*)

What? what?—Is that my body?—Am I dead?

CECILIA.   You seem to be alive.

CECIL.   If feeling be
The test of life, I do live.—And yet that—
(*returning toward the bed and looking at the effigy.*)
That is my body.

CECILIA   (*meeting him as he turns about, and pointing
to his own form*).

Nay, but look you here.—

What then is this?

CECIL   (*placing his hand on his chest*).

This?—'Tis so light, so free!

'Tis but an essence framed of flutterings,

Ethereal as the trillings of a lark
Left up in heaven when it has dropt to earth.—
And you call this a body?
CECILIA.   That one there,
          (*pointing toward the bed.*)
Holds not your thought?
CECIL.   Nay, it has flown to you.
CECILIA.   And wherefore, think you, has it flown to
     me?
CECIL.   I do not know.   It seems as if my soul
Had all my life been flying thus to you.
Why, when you speak, your voice the echo seems
Of some familiar strain, with which all sounds
That ever I thought sweet were in accord.
And when my dimmed eyes dare to face your
     own,
Each seems a sky within which is inframed
A world that holds my lifetime ; and the light
Beams like a sun there, scattering doubt and
     gloom.
          (*looking around.*)
But what a world you live in !—Golden skies?—
Is it the sunset?
CECILIA.   Nay ; you see no sun.
CECIL.   Is it the Indian Summer?
CECILIA.   Nay ; you see
The air is far too clear.
CECIL.   Is there a breeze?—
I feel it fan me.

CECILIA.   Yet the leaves move not.

CECIL.   Why, every leaf glows fairer than a flower !—
It must be autumn.

CECILIA   (*plucking a leaf, and handing it to him*).
                    Nay; these leaves are fresh.

CECIL.   I think I dream :—all things appear so
strange
Yet doubt I dream :—they all appear so clear.

CECILIA   (*sitting on one of the lower steps, leading up
from the stage to the arbor*).
Does nothing seem familiar ?

CECIL   (*sitting, in a half kneeling position, on a step be-
side* CECILIA, *but lower than the one that she
occupies, and gazing up reverentially toward her*).
                    No—yet, yes.
I dimly can recall what now appears
A troubled, stormy sea, yet not a sea ;
And in the depth that which I call myself
Seemed held and heaved as in some diving bell.
But evermore in reveries and dreams,
But most in dreams when outward sense would
sleep
My soul would be released, and rise and reach
Fresh air, in which was breathed what gave fresh
life ;
Then, sinking downward, wake and work again,
Till time for rest and fresh refreshment came.
But never could my powers at work below
Remember aught that blest them when above.

CECILIA. And now you dream that somehow they
    came here?

CECIL. Oh, do not tell me that I now but dream!—
Nay, say 'tis heaven?—Or is the rest of sleep
But absence from the body while we draw
New drafts of life from that which gave us life?

CECILIA. What do you think?

CECIL.   I do not think at all.
I only know I would that I were Adam;
And you were Eve, created while I slept.
Or is it true that all our souls create
The things that they aspire for?—And are you,—
You whom my very spirit seems to clasp
And thrill forever at each tingling touch,
Are you, indeed, the form of my ideal?
Oh, love, you seem as if at one with God;
And yet I never thought a God could be
So dear.

               (kneeling.)
        I've heard of monks in ecstasy
Who saw—or thought they saw—the Virgin. I—
I could not credit them. But now, it seems——

CECILIA. You think that I——

CECIL.   I know not what you are.
I only know my soul has sought for you;
And now has found the search was not in vain.
Why, and how is it that I know so well—
How have you told me—what you are to me?

CECILIA. I have not told you this; and only He

Who formed the spirit knows the how and why.
CECIL.   Who formed?—Why, that is God. I
   thought me dead.
Yet here, I see not——
            (*gazing around and upward.*)
CECILIA.   You had hoped, at death,
   To pass to Paradise, and be at rest.
   Move on : I have detained you.
      (*rising, and waving him off with gesture.*)
CECIL (*rising anxiously*).
                          I move on ?—
   And you stay here ?—I cannot.   There is not
   The littlest finger of the littlest nerve
   In all my frame here, that could summon power
   To move where you moved not.
CECILIA.   Ah, then your will
   Is mightier than you deemed it ?   You can rise
   But when you wish to rise ?   The gates of heaven
   Need not be closed to keep you out of them ?
(*seating herself on a step higher than she occupied be-
            fore.*)
CECIL (*sitting beside, but below her*).
   Keep out of them ?—Why, your sweet form alone
   Has brought me now a million, million times
   More than I ever dreamed that death could bring
      me.
CECILIA.   But where is your religion ?
CECIL.   All was love.—
CECILIA.   And not the Christ—?

CECIL. Why, yes—that which he was—
For which he died,—the spirit in the man,—
In me, in you.—Ah, now it seems as if
Each face I loved on earth but imaged yours !—
Why is it, dear one, that you seem to be
So fully all things that they all could be?
And what love is it ?—what, the halo here
That seems to orb you in the sphere of God ?
CECILIA.   Had you seen more of that, you might
find out.
CECIL.   I would I could !
CECILIA (*rising, as does also* CECIL).
                    And shall I help you to it ?
CECIL.   I knew there was no wish within my soul
That would not find an echo in your own.
Where shall we go that we may find—?
CECILIA (*pointing toward the Right*).   You see
Those coming ?—Let us watch them first—from
here.
          (*They enter the arbor, where, in view of the
          audience, they overlook the stage.
          Enter—Right—*LOWE *and* MADAM LOWE *in
          gray Quaker costumes, resembling in most
          regards those of* CECIL *and* CECILIA.
          (*Blue-gray light illumines the stage.*)
CECIL (*aside*).
     They look like Lowe, the Quaker, and his wife.
LOWE (*to* MADAM L.).
     I feel so weary, yet we hoped for rest.

MADAM L. (*to* LOWE).
   Did I not walk with thee, I half might doubt
   The leading of this path.
LOWE.   I doubt it not,
   When leading thee.—Who ever saw thee decked
   In vain attire ?
MADAM L.   Or thee not grave and gray ?
LOWE.   Or heard thee romp ?
MADAM L.   Or thee hilarious ?
LOWE.   Or found thee once the toy of giddy fancy ?
MADAM L.   Or thee, of disconcerted calculation ?
LOWE.   None ever !—Yet I fear this path.—I
      thought
   I heard—and Oh, I dared to listen twice !—
   I thought I heard strange singing —
MADAM L.   Birds ?—I thought
   I saw—and Oh, I dared to look there twice !—
   I thought I saw a wicked, grinning ape.
LOWE.   Hush, hush ! Think not of these things.
      Nay, but think
   Of things that God hath made.—I wonder if
                  (*becoming shrewd*)
   The holy city be completely built.
MADAM L.   They might give thee a contract.
LOWE.   Well, they might !
   And if the saints be not all Friends——
MADAM L.   Sh—sh—
   Not that !—so loud !—I fear me lest 'tis doubt.
LOWE.   To doubt is charity, where to believe

Is to condemn. Who knows but we could thrive
Deprived of friends—build churches.
MADAM L. Say not that.
We may be taken down yet, where they use them.
LOWE. I fear me some may use them here. For
    look !—
(*Part of the stage is illuminated with red light.*)
The colors on the leaves, the very skies
Seem sadly gay.
MADAM L. Oh, do not look at them !
They glow to tempt the lusting of the eye.
LOWE. Sh, sh !—What's that ? Loud noise and
    music too !
(BLAVER *and* MISS PRIMWOOD *are heard singing.*)

Oh, up and spout, and down and shout,
And show the spirit off and out.

MADAM L. Oh, there may be a fiend here ! Let
    us hide.
*Exeunt—Right Third—*LOWE *and* MADAM L. *hur-
    riedly.*

    *Enter—Left Upper—*BLAVER *and* MISS PRIM-
    WOOD *in blue clothes resembling those of*
    CECIL *and* CECILIA. *Stage is illumined
    with dark blue light.*

CECIL (*aside*).
They're Blaver and Miss Primwood, I should
    say.

BLAVER. We should have found the place ere
    this ; or heard
The blowing of the trumpets, or the shouts——
MISS P. Of all the deacons, yes.
BLAVER.   We soon shall reach
    The place " where congregations ne'er break
        up."—
    Oh, I could talk forever !
MISS P.   So could I !—
    Yet,—do you know ?—if I were not with you,
    I half should tremble, lest my feet were near
    The silence of the——
BLAVER (*in a frightened way*).
                Do not speak of that !
    Keep talking.—It's too true !—There's not **one**
      shout.
    There's no one got the power here.
MISS P.   It may be,
    They all have got it.
BLAVER.   What if that were so ?—
    Suppose they had.—Suppose that no one here
    Could ever find a spirit to reform—
    Not one to preach to,—how could saints here
      know
    About one's gifts ?
MISS P. (*agitated*).
             Yes, yes ; but keep on talking.
    To be with one who talks on, makes one sure
    The silence is not near.

BLAVER. I'll talk. You sing.
Perhaps, at times, to change a tune or text,
The congregation pauses ; and may hear,
And send the sexton for us.

Enter—Right Third—stealthily, and dodging behind
trees, LOWE *and* MADAM L.

MISS P. (*pointing toward the Right*).
Who are they,
So still, so backward, skulking through the trees ?
BLAVER. So backward and so still !—They're both
bad signs.
MISS P. Though this were Paradise, there might
be here
Another serpent.
BLAVER. Or those like him !—Would
Be backward too, and not stand up for aught.
MISS P. Would slip away.
BLAVER. Be still in doing it.
MISS P. (*clinging to* BLAVER'S *arm*).
How glad I am I learned to be a woman,
And cling to man ! Ah, were I here alone——
BLAVER. Those two seem slipping just like
drunken sneaks
Evading prohibition laws.—I have it :
Heaven's recognized my mission. How they'll
quail
When I exhort them ! But what's more religious
Than ministering discomfort ? Rile folks up,
6

Their dregs appear.   They're conscious in their
   depths.

You watch them now.—Hoho ! hoho ! hoho !

(BLAVER *is gesturing toward the Right Third En-*
     trance.)

     *Enter—Right Upper Entrance—*FATHER HY-
     CHER, *and* WIDOW HYCHER, *in red clothes*
     resembling those of CECIL *and* CECILIA
     save that the FATHER *has a clerical ap-*
     pearance.   The stage is suddenly illumined
     with red light.

FATHER H. (*to* BLAVER).

Hold, preaching fiend !   How dare you block my
   path

And raise that impious and schismatic shout ?

Down on your knees.

(*then to* LOWE *and* MADAM LOWE, *who appear at the*
     Right).

          Down on your knees.

MADAM LOWE.   Vain souls,

Trained on the earth to influence souls through
   force,

In realms where spirits have not forms that force

Can harm, must find their occupation gone.

*Exeunt—Right Third—*LOWE *and* MADAM LOWE.

CECIL (*aside, as he looks at the two who have just*
     arrived).

Father and Widow Hycher, or their doubles !—

The Quaker lady's not forgot her training.

BLAVER (*to* MISS PRIMWOOD, *as his eye follows* MADAM LOWE).

Expected to surprise her !—Failed !—She knows
The devil's never naked—wears a mask—
And robes.

MISS P. (*to* BLAVER, *anxiously*).

But should he——

BLAVER (*to* MISS P.).

He said " preaching fiend."
The one that rails at preaching, proves he needs it.
How red he is !—He drinks—fire-water, eh ?

MISS P. I fear so ; yes.

WIDOW H. (*to* BLAVER).

He bade you kneel.

BLAVER (*to* WIDOW H.). I'm not
His suitor—No ; nor yours. You two don't suit
me.

WIDOW H. (*advancing in a menacing way, and pointing toward the Right, but incidentally also toward* FATHER H.).

'Tis time you go to——

BLAVER. You go there yourself.
Oh, 'twill be missionary work for you !
I'll not be tempted that way, then.

MISS P. (*to* WIDOW H., *and pointing toward* BLAVER).

Not he !—
He's not for women's rights !

BLAVER (*to* MISS P.'s *querying*).

Who is, that's here ?

MISS P. (*to* BLAVER, *pointing toward* FATHER H. *and*
    WIDOW H.).
Those women.
BLAVER (*pointing to* FATHER H.).
                He's no woman.
MISS P.   Then is he
For men's rights?
BLAVER (*laughingly*) Humph! Frocks uniform his
    calling;
His calling represents both men and women;
So he—he tries to take from each their best;
And thinks the woman's best is in her gown!—
But isn't it somewhat strange so many forms
We meet in Paradise should seem to garb
Our worst aversions?
MISS P. (*with solicitude*).   Very!—Yet do not
Leave off exhorting them!
BLAVER (*to* FATHER *and* WIDOW H.).
                    Hoho! hoho!
WIDOW H. (*to* FATHER H.).
I feel as if some storm were near, and yet
Were blowing music for me.
FATHER H. (*to* WIDOW H.).
                    Heard in heaven,
Storms blowing from the mouth of hell make
    music.
MISS P. (*to* BLAVER, *looking toward* WIDOW H.)
There, there, I say. That woman wants her
    rights.

BLAVER (*to* Miss P.).

She'll get them soon enough just where she is.

You know, I think I've talked to him before.

There were those never influenced — always thought

It was the devil. — Now, you see, we've proved it.

FATHER H. (*to* BLAVER *to whom he advances*).

Tell me, foul, shouting fiend ; for surely thou

Hast felt his vengeance on thy damnéd soul,

Where dwelleth the most high Inquisitor ?

BLAVER (*to* FATHER H.).

I'm no inquisitor myself; so never

Have made inquiry. Let the like seek like.

MISS P. (*to* BLAVER).

His thunder sounds like music which one hears,

Yet need not, if he wish not.

(FATHER H. *talks aside to* WIDOW H.)

BLAVER (*to* MISS P.). 'Tis his color—

The red of it—that flags the foe for me. .

A chance, at last, to show what one can do !

And, oh, I tell you, 'twould be just like nature

To fling this chip, when clearing out its workshop,

Down toward the fire,—that we might exercise

Our gifts upon it, blow and blow and blow,

(FATHER *and* WIDOW HYCHER *disappear behind a rock or tree at the Right*).

And either set the spark to burning more,

Or put it out. So now's our time—Hoho !

Hoho ! hoho ! hoho ! —

(*noticing that the* HYCHERS *have disappeared*).

        Why, where 've they gone ?—

Skulked off ?—We might have known they would.

We'll follow.

You sing, and I will shout.

      (*Moves toward Right*).

MISS P.   Not that way, **no** !

     (*Both turn to the Left*).

BLAVER and MISS P. (*together*).

  Hoho ! hoho ! hoho ! hoho !

  We've all things here you need to know.

   *Exeunt—Left—*BLAVER *and* MISS PRIMWOOD.

(*Reappear at the Right,* FATHER HYCHER *and* WIDOW

      HYCHER).

WIDOW H. If I were not with you, I half might

  fear

That we had wholly missed the narrow path,

But with my shepherd near me, all is well.

FATHER H. 'Tis odd, indeed, that I've not found a

  flock,

Nor sheepfold, not a single hedge, forsooth,

In which to drive a single soul.

WIDOW H.   Like that—

Where all were kept so safe—no schism there !—

The walls were always echoing back the words

You spoke ; and no one else was let to speak.

FATHER H. All heard what they believed.

WIDOW H.   Could they do else
Than to believe what they were always hearing ?—
Dear words, how we must thank them for our
   faith !

FATHER H. Without our words men might be
   left to nature.

WIDOW H.   Just think of that !—And where would
   nature bear them ?

FATHER H.   Off from the church, I fear.

WIDOW H.   Yes, yes, and off—
Off from the priest.

FATHER H.   From God, as well.

WIDOW H.   Of course.
For He is so unnatural.

FATHER H.   You mean
Is supernatural.

WIDOW H.   Mysterious !—
Creates our reason, yet condemns its use.
I never used my reason—did not dare.

FATHER H.   You were a model woman, always,
   yes.

WIDOW H.   And you a model man—no monk with
   me ;
Yet always showed the world a pious face.

FATHER H.   I did.   They lied who said I did not
   care
For truth.   How oft, for it, I held my tongue !

WIDOW H.   And so held on to it.

FATHER H.   And kept it sacred.

WIDOW H.   And easy too for us, who need not
  find it.
For my part, I would rather have no truth
Than risk damnation, planning how to use it.
How kind the priest to do our thinking for us,
And make us, through not thinking, think just
  right !
FATHER H.   But you did thinking—thought of me.
WIDOW H.   Of course,
  When you thought for me.—Is that what you
  wished?
And now, that we are here, you'll think for me?
FATHER H.   Could I do else ?
WIDOW H.   And when we reach the gates,
  You'll promise not to leave me ; for, you know,
  I've never learned the language of the spirit;
  And might not know it, were you not beside me.
FATHER H.   I—yes—but if——
WIDOW H.   There was no *if* in what
  You used to say.
*Exeunt—Left—*FATHER HYCHER *and* WIDOW HY-
          CHER.
        (*The red light changes to golden, and* CECIL
          and CECILIA *come out from the arbor,
          and, while speaking, gradually descend to
          the stage.*)
CECIL.   They did not see us.
CECILIA.   No
  For they did not look up.

CECIL. I know, but why?—
Where all things round them were so new and
strange?
CECILIA. The spirit is the slave of its desire.
They did not care to look above themselves.
CECIL. Pray tell me who they were. They seemed
so near,
And yet so many million miles away.
They looked like people, too, whom once I
knew;
Yet moved like cuckoos jointed on a clock,
Accenting nothing they have thought themselves,
Or have the force to make another think of.
CECILIA. They seemed to be lost souls.
CECIL (*startled*).

Lost souls, you say?
CECILIA. Did you not note them—how they wan-
dered on;
Nor knew their destination?
CECIL. Heaven forbid!
CECILIA. Why pray for this?—You think that force
rules here,—
That spirits are not free to wander where
Their own ideals bear them?
CECIL. Those they formed
On earth, you mean?
CECILIA. Where else could they be formed?
CECIL. And whither, think you, will ideals bear
Those whom we just have seen?

CECILIA. Where would you deem
These could be realized—save on the earth?

CECIL. But some of them seemed seeking for their
Christ.

CECILIA. I fear those seeking only for their Christ
May sometimes fail to find the Christ of God.

CECIL. But will they never find Him?

CECILIA. Do you think
That those in search but for a false ideal,
Could recognize Him, even should they find
Him?

CECIL. Is not the Christ of God in all the
churches?

CECILIA. Is He not preached through men?

CECIL. And are not men
Controlled?—inspired?

CECILIA. And, if so, from what source?
Are there no spirits in the line between
Divinity and man?—And what of man,—
This urn of earth in which the true seed falls?—
There was an Arab in Mohammed's time;
In Joan of Arc's, there was a maid of France.

CECIL. But would you grant their claim?

CECILIA. Some keen as you
Believed it true. And is it charity
To deem them dupes?

CECIL. But one must deem them this,
Or call upon their prophets.

CECILIA. Think you so?

You've heard of gypsies telling what came true.
Did this truth prove them seers of highest truth?
Believe not every spirit; prove——
CECIL.   But how?
CECILIA.   How but by what is said, and character
Of him who says it?   To the true soul, truth
Appeals to taste, as beauty to the sense;
Its test is quality.   The truth of Christ
Is proved by traits of Christ.   The like comes
    from like.
Their inspiration is the nearest God
Whose lives and loves are nearest Him.
CECIL.   May those
Not near Him be inspired too?
CECILIA.   Why may not
Some lower phase of spirit-power, earth-trained
To live for matter only, still intent
To live for matter, take abode in them,
And work its will upon their willing souls?
What difference whether men may rise on earth
Impelled through emulation to enforce
Their wills on others; or, through appetite
May fall, and yield control of reason's reins
To that which drives them on to lust and crime?—
A spirit that inspires through selfishness
To mean success or failure, equally
May vex as by a devil made incarnate
Oneself and all about him.
CECIL.   Poor weak man!

Enter—Left—FREEMAN *and* FAITH, *dressed like* CECIL *and* CECILIA.

CECILIA. Weak always—save when conscious of his need.

FREEMAN (*advancing, speaking to the two, and pointing toward the Right Rear*).

Does this path lead us upward?

CECILIA.   Yes, it does.

FREEMAN (*looking at* CECIL, *and speaking to him*).

Why, why, friend, is this you?

          (*to* CECILIA.)

                   And Celia too?—

CECILIA. You'll find us friends, at least, whoe'er we be.

(CECIL *and* CECILIA *shake hands with* FREEMAN *and* FAITH.)

CECIL (*to* FREEMAN).

And Freeman, you're with Faith?—I join your joy.
Why, it fulfills my dream for you.

FREEMAN.   And mine!

(*to* FAITH, *and gesturing toward their surroundings.*)

How much, with each new step, th' horizon widens.

FAITH. How could one bide below!

FREEMAN (*thoughtfully, and pointing toward the Left*).

                 Ask Father Hycher.

FAITH. And he was such a good and learnéd man!

FREEMAN. Less good than learnéd, darling. Your pure soul
Breathed such an atmosphere about itself

Your very presence could impart an air
Of sacredness to all brought near to you.
FAITH.   Well, now the father interests me not;
Nor she that held the place of mother to me.
FREEMAN (*pointing upward*).
Those interest us now who call us upward.
FAITH (*to* CECILIA, *while* FREEMAN *turns to* CECIL).
'Tis wondrous how much wiser and more wide
His views appear to be here than the Father's—
Who was so learnéd !
CECILIA.   Wondrous, does it seem ?
Why so ?—Though spirit-life be lived in thought,
Where thought pervades the atmosphere like
    air,
What can its measure be, for any mind,
Save that mind's receptivity?   If so,
When freed from bounds conditioning human
    thought,
'Tis not a filled.mind but an open mind,
Where waits not bigotry but charity,
Although with little learning, that first thrills
To tides that flow from infinite resources.
FREEMAN (*who has turned to listen to the latter
    part of what she has been saying*).
Is this a revelation ?
CECILIA.   'Tis to those
Who heed the truth behind the words I use ;
And yet to those who heed this truth themselves
I do not need to say 'tis revelation.

FREEMAN. We'll move on then, and test it for
ourselves.

Farewell, kind friends, until we meet above.

(FREEMAN *and* FAITH *shake hands with* CECIL *and*
CECILIA).

CECILIA. Farewell.

CECIL. Farewell.

(FREEMAN *and* FAITH *pass upward through, or around
the arbor, till, finally they disappear.*)

*Exeunt—Back Center—*FREEMAN *and* FAITH.

CECIL (*looking at them as they ascend*).

Oh, happy, blessed pair !

(*The following is then chanted by the choir,
either invisible, or visible at the rear of the
stage. During the singing,* CECILIA *and*
CECIL *gradually ascend to the arbor where
both sit.*

Two springs of life,—in air and earth ;
  Two tides,—in soul and sod ;
Two natures,—wrought of breath and birth ;
  Two aims,—in cloud and clod ;—
Oh, where were worlds, or where were worth
  Without the two, and God ?

Two movements in the heaving breast,
  Two, in the beating heart ;
Two, in the swaying soldier's crest ;
  Two, in the strokes of art ;—
Oh where in aught of mortal quest,
  Are e'er the two apart ?

Two times of day,—in gloom and glow;
  Two realms—of dream and deed;
Two seasons—bringing sod and snow;
  Two states—of fleshed and freed;—
Oh where is it that life would go,
  But through the two they lead?

Two frames that meet,—the strong, the fair,
  True love in both begun;
Two souls that form a single pair;
  Two courses both have run;—
Oh where is life in earth or air,
  And not with these at one?

CECIL (*pointing in the direction taken by* FREEMAN *and* FAITH).
And now they rest?
CECILIA.   Why not?   What now remains
Of an ideal to bear them back to earth?—
Or what to learn from mortals?
CECIL.   Learn from mortals?
Can mortals aid immortals?
CECILIA.   Life is one.
The day's toil gives one sweeter dreams at night;
And sweeter dreams more strength for daily toil.
If thought may pass from sphere to sphere, why
    not
The benefit of thought?
CECIL.   Why, this were strange!
CECILIA.   If strangeness were a test of what is false,
Few things would be believed that were not true.

CECIL.   But high and heavenly spirits helped by
     human ?
CECILIA.   Why should not all in heaven or earth be
     helped
   By all with whom in spirit they are one ?
   Were you on earth, the while your soul aspired,
   Could mine not move up with you?   What you
     learned,
   Could it not ever be a part of me ?
CECIL.   Why, this is that for which I so have
     longed !
   And once with one I thought that I had found it.
   Ah, can it be the halo crowning her,
   Was your sweet face behind the face I saw ?—
   Yet—were it right to turn from her to you ?
CECILIA.   All ties are right that make true life more
     bright.
   Think you that she had not her own ideal ?
          (*gesturing toward the Right.*)
   And were her soul but free to pass to it,
   Do you imagine she would pass to you ?
CECIL (*looking toward the Right*).
   My wife   with   Kraft?—How   can   it   be?—and
     yet——

(*The stage is suddenly illumined with brown light.*)

     Enter—Left—Right — KRAFT *and* MADAM
       CECIL, *dressed in dark brown clothes,*
       shaped like those of CECIL *and* CELIA.

MADAM CECIL (*to* KRAFT).   It matters not what we
    have done.   Have faith.

KRAFT (*to* MADAM CECIL *with suppressed fear*).

    But should I meet my wife whose will I broke,

    Whose slaves were not set free——

MADAM C.   Have faith, have faith !

KRAFT.   Or should we two meet Cecil——

MADAM C. (*in abject fear*).

                    Oh, oh, oh,

    Speak not of that !   'Tis paid, I say.   Have
    faith.

KRAFT (*doubtingly*).

    Yet some would talk of proving faith by works.

MADAM C.   I joined the church when I was sweet
    sixteen,

    And never danced, except away from home.

KRAFT.   And I, when I was twenty ; and I never
    Let others see me backslide.

MADAM C.   And I always

    Appeared to take an interest in the meetings.

KRAFT.   And I would often head subscription
    lists

    With more than one could pay, when they were
    due.

MADAM C.   Yes, we were both consistent and dis-
    creet.

KRAFT.   But yet, should we meet Cecil——

MADAM C. (*shuddering*).

              Oh, oh, oh,

7

Not him ! not him !
    (*recovering herself suddenly.*)
        He never can come here.
KRAFT (*eagerly*).
  You think so—eh ?—Why not ?
MADAM C. (*sententiously*).
        He lost his faith.
KRAFT (*with cringing hope*).
  Is that so ?—Yes ?—but how ?
MADAM C.   Why, just because
  Our pastor said, one time, of slavery,
  The institution was divine, God's own,
  He never after set foot in that church.
KRAFT (*with self-congratulatory delight*).
  Oh, is that so !
MADAM C.   Besides, he sometimes owned
  To other——
KRAFT.   Other what?
MADAM C.   Misgivings.
KRAFT (*with assumed horror*).
                Not
  Believe in things men preached ?
MADAM C. (*sanctimoniously*).
        He doubted them.
KRAFT (*decisively*).
  Then he did not have faith.
MADAM C.   No ; he did not.
KRAFT. I learned the catechism in my youth ;
  And, when men asked me, always said 'twas true.

Madam C. Thank God for that! He was not
trained as you were.

Kraft. You know I would not let an ignorant
man,

A slave or poor white, meet me in my parlor.

Madam C. Of course not !

Kraft. How can one who's ignorant
About the doctrines—doubts them,—how can he
Expect that God will welcome him?

Madam C. Just so !
We never have a God we understand
Until we learn to judge Him by ourselves.

> (Cecilia, *beckoning to* Cecil *who follows her,
> comes from the arbor, and moves toward*
> Kraft *and* Madam C., *who, being at the
> front of the stage facing the audience, do
> not see them.*)

Kraft (*in self-congratulatory way*).

Your husband then had really lost his faith?

I wonder if my wife had not lost hers.

Madam C. Did she not free her slaves?—Our
pastor said

The institution was divine.

Kraft (*deliberatingly*).
Yes, yes.

Madam C. She did not think it so.

Kraft. No, she did not.

But I, I did, you see. I broke her will.

Madam C. Precisely !

KRAFT.   Yes.

MADAM C.   And saved her.—

KRAFT.   What?—Oh, yes!—
Saved her from the results——

CECILIA (*to* KRAFT *and* MADAM C., *as she points to*
    CECIL).

                         What sophistry
    Is this?

MADAM C. (*falling on her knees before* CECIL, *in
    abject fear*).

              Oh, Master, did I not have faith?

KRAFT (*also falling on his knees before* CECIL).
    Did I not often say "Good Lord" in prayer?

MADAM C.   Did I not do my best to show myself
    In church?

KRAFT.   Did I not make professions there?

MADAM C.   Did I not bear my cross?—

KRAFT.   A diamond cross
    I gave her?—

MADAM C.   I embroidered one.   I showed
    My faith by works.

KRAFT.   I, in my business,—
    Oh, how my slaves would work at those church
        fairs!

CECIL (*to* CECILIA).
    Are they insane?

CECILIA.   In part.

CECIL.   Heard you the name
    They called us?

CECILIA. His who said that " Inasmuch
As ye have done it to the least of these,
My brethren, ye have done it unto Me."
MADAM C. Oh, Master, wherefore are we here?
CECIL (*to* CECILIA).

Where do
They think themselves?
CECILIA. Where false and hellish moods
Create a false and hellish world to live in.
CECIL (*to* KRAFT *and* MADAM C.).
What seems the trouble? What is it you fear?
KRAFT. Oh, Master!
MADAM C. Master!
CECIL. Why do you say that?
MADAM C. You are so holy, and we are so base.
KRAFT. Oh, wherefore did I kill you?
MADAM C. Wherefore, oh,
Oh, wherefore did I load you with abuse?—
I did not know you then.
CECIL. Nor know me now.
Am I your master?
KRAFT. It was you we harmed.
CECIL. What would you that I do for you?
MADAM C. Oh let
Us pay it back.
KRAFT. Yes, let us pay it back.
CECILIA. Pay what back? Said you not just now,
" 'Tis paid.

Have faith." Your faith means faith that God
    forgives.
If he forgive you, why not feel forgiven ?
MADAM C.   You mock us.
KRAFT.   Mock us.
CECIL (*to* CECILIA).

                    Tell me what to say.
And is there nothing one can do for them
To free them from their misery ?
CECILIA.   They say
    There is, and truly.   Though the Lord forgive,
    In spirit how can spirits feel forgiven
    Ere they undo the wrong their lives have wrought ?
    Ere this had been undone, not even laws
    Of Moses let the trespasser receive
    The benefit of sacrifice ; and how
    Could heavenly joys crown even perfect love
    Save as it served the soul it once had harmed ?
CECIL (*to* MADAM C. *and* KRAFT).

    What is it, then, that you would do for me ?
KRAFT.   What you had done, had we not stayed
    your work.
CECIL (*to* CECILIA).

    What ?—Is it possible ?—my plans, my hopes
    Can be fulfilled yet ? and fulfilled. through these ?—
            (*to* KRAFT *and* MADAM C.)
    Well, it may be so.   You may serve your time.
MADAM C.   Ah, now I know, indeed, that Heaven
    is true !

KRAFT. And now I know, indeed, the Lord forgives!

CECILIA. But prove your faith by your fidelity.

> (CECILIA *points toward the Right Third En-*
> *trance. As she does so, Enter—Right*
> *Upper Entrance—*JEM *and* MILLY. *Their*
> *dresses are of a grayer shade, but other-*
> *wise they resemble those of* CECIL *and* CE-
> CILIA. *As* KRAFT *and* MADAM C. *turn*
> *toward the Right Third Entrance, they*
> *see* JEM *and* MILLY. *Both start back*
> *affrighted.*)

MADAM C. See those grim messengers of torture
coming!

CECIL (*to* CECILIA).

Why, those are Jem and Milly, our old slaves!
She tried to thwart me, when I set them free.

CECILIA. She thinks them fiends.

CECIL.   How blind! Their dusky hues
To me seem fair as shadows cast before
The love of coming angels.

> (CECILIA *and* CECIL, *at her apparent bidding,*
> *seat themselves again on some of the steps*
> *leading up to the arbor, and from there*
> *listen to the following.*)

MADAM C. (*to* JEM *and* MILLY, *kneeling before them*).
                    Spare my soul!

JEM. A little thing to spare!—I 'spects I will.

MADAM C. You will not drive me off to torment
then?

JEM. Come, come, ole missus, you's mixed up on
      dis.
      De debil's not so black as he am painted.
      He'm white,—a missus too! When you gets dah,
                    (*pointing down.*)
      Jes' take one look in dat ah lake. You'll see 'im.
MADAM C. Oh, oh, then you have seen him?
JEM.   Rather reckon!
      'Cause I's been down below,—a slave, you sees.
      But now, I's free.
MADAM C.   And I must be your slave?
JEM. No ; we's not mean enough to own no slaves,
                 (*Gesturing toward* MILLY.)
MADAM C. But you'll not drive us to the darkness?
JEM.   No.
      We's come away from dah, or 'spected so
      Till we met——
                 (JEM *looks at her sharply.*)
MADAM C.   Who? Oh, take me not——
JEM.   For him ?—
      No, I will not. You's kneelin'.
MADAM C.   I will serve
      For all my life——
JEM.   De debil ?—better not!
(JEM *and* MILLY *turn to leave at Right Third
                 Entrance.*)
MADAM C. I must pay back the service forced
          from you.
      You will not, cannot, must not cast me off.

JEM (*turning around toward her*).
Dem folks dat's free prefer to choose deir help.
*Exeunt—Right Third Entrance—*JEM *and* MILLY, *hurriedly.*
MADAM C. (*to* KRAFT *who seems to desire to linger*).
Oh, we must overtake them !
(*She pulls* KRAFT *after her.*)
*Exeunt—Right Third Entrance—*MADAM C. *and* KRAFT.
(*As they leave, the stage is again illumined with golden light.*)
CECILIA (*looking after them*).
                  Who can tell
What ages it may take to overtake
The wrong one's own wrong lashes into flight !
CECIL.   Where are they going ?
CECILIA.   Earthward, so it seems.
CECIL.   And will she serve her slaves ?
CECILIA.   Why should she not ?
Why should not those who were the most oppressed
Have most to serve them where the soul is served ?
All things inverted and turned inside out,
The last in station may become the first,
The lowly lordlike and the high the low,
The crown'd the chain'd, the crucified the crown'd.
CECIL.   But how and where can spirits right their wrong ?

CECILIA. Wherever spirit influences spirit.

CECIL. Ah, then, through others' lives they work
   their work?

CECILIA. Perchance they may; perchance they
   may do more.

CECIL. Do more?—What mean you?—live again
   on earth?—
   Nay, if they shall, they have lived; yet who ever
   Met mortal yet whose memory could recall
   A former state?

CECILIA. He might recall a state
   Without its circumstance. To know, bespeaks
   Experience. To be born with intuitions
   And insight, is to know. To sun new growth,
   Why should not all be given an equal chance
   Unshadow'd by dark memories of the past?

CECIL. But if the past were bright?

CECILIA. If wholly so,
   Would one need progress? or could he be cursed
   With deeper woe than thought that could recall,
   Enslaved in flesh, a former liberty?
   Why tempt to suicide, that, breaking through
   The lines determining development,
   May plunge the essence down to deeper depths
   There planted till new growth take root anew?

CECIL. Must all new growth be planted in the
   earth?

CECILIA. Is any germ that grows not planted
   there?

CECIL.   What trains it then ?

CECILIA.   'Tis said that where it falls,
In age, clime, country, family, fleshly form,
The mighty wheels of matter—earth and moon,
And sun and planets, all the unseen stars
Of all the universe that round it roll—
With one unending whirl grind out its fate ;
Yet only earthly fate.   Tossed to and fro,
And torn by care and toil and pain and loss,
The spirit knows in spirit it is free ;
And, true to its high nature, may pass through
The terror of the ordeal with all
The finer flour of nature's grain preserved.

CELIA.   So though careers are fated, souls are free ?

CECIL.   The consciousness of freedom comes from
      force
Which is of heaven ; the consciousness of fate
From that which is of earth ; and both are true ;
Or that which makes all feel them both is false.

CECIL.   But if some spirits thus return to earth,
Why not all spirits ?

CECILIA.   Who has traced for you
The history of spirits ?   If they came
From God, as matter came, why came they not
With matter?

CECIL.   What ?—Through beasts and birds, you
      mean ?

CECILIA.   Why not?—Why should not these have
      endless life ?

Why, if they have it, should their course be
 checked
Ere they attain the highest ?—and, if not,
Why should their essence not move up through
 man ?
CECIL. Is man the son of beasts ?
CECILIA.   In flesh why not ?—
But may be born of flesh and of the Spirit.
Devoid of spirit, all the body's nerves
Are lifeless as the wires, when rent apart,
Which once were thrilling with electric force.
But ah ! that force, though flown to air, comes
 back
To give new life wherever new forms fit it.
So, while the whole creation of the flesh,
In groans and travails of successive births,
Prepares each new formation for its need,
Why should not psychic force, the breath of Him
In whom all live and move and have their being,
With rhythm mightier than the pulse of lungs,
Or day and night, or autumn and the spring,
Pass up through all the lower ranks of life.
Through birth and on through death, from air to
 breath,
From breath to air, till, last, it reaches man ;
And, taught the lesson there of human hands
Which give a mastery over matter, make
A fellow worker in creation's work,
And of the human voice which, framing words

To hold each new conception in control,
Imparts a mastery over mind, and makes
A fellow-thinker in creation's thought,—
Why should not this force, moulded by the hand
And head. attain in man its final end,
And dowered with will and reason, freed at death
From its material framework, hold its mould,
And reach the last result of all that is,
Where that which served the serpent is the son,—
A spirit in the image of the Father?

CECIL. These words recall an ancient eastern
 dream;
And, in one's waking hours, can it be true?

CECILIA. Think you a true soul ever served a
 thought
Not souled in truth, whatever were its form?

CECIL. But what then of the Christ?

CECILIA.   Did He not say
He lived in spirit ere He lived on earth?—

CECIL. He said He came for others.

CECILIA.   Do you think
A spirit such as His would need to come
For His own gooa?

CECIL.   And yet His sacrifice?—

CECILIA. He sacrificed the spirit-life for life
On earth, and life on earth for spirit-life.

CECIL. And but fulfilled a common rôle?

CECILIA.   Not common,
Did He fulfill our spirit's best ideal;

For spirits live in thought.   How can they know
Of any God beyond their thought of Him ?
CECIL.   But if they know His Son ?
CECILIA.   They know, at best,
A " Son of Man," as well as " Son of God,"—
In spirit one with Him, but not in frame.
CECIL.   And yet a " Saviour "—
CECILIA.   What inspires, but spirit ?—
Or saves, but inspiration ?   He—enough—
All must move upward would they find the Christ.
          (*Rising and pointing upward.*)
CECIL (*rising*).
But ought they not to work for others too ?
CECILIA.   In spirit those work most for truth, who
     most
Are true ; for all are led, yet all are leaders.
Thus does the line of being bridge the gulf
Between the world of worm and fire,—the hell
Forever following life not saved on earth,—
And that eternal rest where souls, made free
From longer craving a material frame
Through which to signal their vain selfhood, lose
Their lower life to find a higher life,
Where now their spirits are at one with that
Whose love creates but that it may bestow ;
And, even as the Christ is in the Father,
So, too, become joint heirs with Him of all things.
(CECILIA *and* CECIL *move upward, and finally dis-
               appear.*)

*Exeunt—Back Center—*Cecilia *and* Cecil. *In the meantime, the following is chanted by a choir, either invisible or visible at the rear of the stage.*

In the world of care and sorrow
　Cloud and darkness shroud the way,
But in heaven there waits a morrow
　Where the night will yield to day,
Where the spirit-light in rising,
　Yet will gild the clouds of fear,
And the shadows, long disguising,
　Lift and leave the landscape clear.

When the soul, amid that glory,
　Finds its earthly garments fall,
Harm and anguish end their story,
　Health and beauty come to all ;
No more fleshly chains can fetter
　Faith that longs to soar above;
None to duty seems a debtor,
　And the only law is love.

There is ended earthly scheming,
　Earthly struggle sinks to sleep ;
Souls have passed from deed to dreaming,
　And they have no watch to keep ;
For the world has wrought its mission,
　And the wheels of labor rest ;
And the faithful find fruition,
　And the true become the blest.

(*The stage is darkened ; and the curtain that formed the back of Scene First in this Act falls upon it.*)

SCENE THIRD. *Same as Scene First of this Act.*
While the stage is still dark, unseen by audience,
    Enter — Left Second Entrance — CECIL, *in*
      dressing-gown covering completely the dress
      worn by him in the last scene. He re-
      clines on the bed, as in the First Scene of
      this Act.
      (The stage is made light.)
    *Enter—Left Second Entrance—*CELIA, *dressed*
      as in Scene First of this Act. In addition,
      she brings a hat and shawl, which, as she
      becomes visible to audience, she is seen
      putting on.

CELIA (*arranging her hat and shawl*).
'Tis time for me to take my morning walk.
I almost fear to leave him !
    *Enter—Right Second Entrance—*JEM.
        (*to* JEM).
             You will stay
While I am gone, and keep good watch of him ?
JEM. Yes, Missus, don't you feah.
    *Exit—Left Second Entrance—*CELIA.
  (JEM *looks out after her, then shuts door.*)
             I'll watch and pway.
I'll watch for dem,
  (*pointing toward Right Second Entrance.*)
          And pway for dis yeah niggah.
Dey wouldn't dare to hahm de Massa now.

What dey would hahm, did I say no, am me.

(*He goes to Right Second Entrance, and opens door, saying*),

Now you'll be safe enough. She 'ab gone away.

Enter — Right Second Entrance — KRAFT, MADAM CECIL and two MEN, all dressed in out-door costume. All of them except KRAFT cross the stage toward the couch. KRAFT remains behind, and, taking a bank-note from his pocket-book, says to himself.

KRAFT. I'm used to courts, and understand the use

Of what they term court-plaster. There is nothing

Can stick together lips inclined to peach

Like strong bank-notes. Here, Jem.

(JEM *moves toward him*, KRAFT *hands him the note.*)

See here. Take this.

It ought to keep your mouth shut.

JEM (*taking money and pocketing it*).

Ay, ay, Massa,

And pocket, too, sah.

KRAFT. You are wise, my man.

(KRAFT *crosses to alcove where* MADAM C. *and the two* MEN *have been looking at* CECIL. *He looks at* CECIL, *and speaks to them.*)

No doubt !—You see the man is living still.

You both can swear to that ?

8

First Man.   Oh, yes.
Second Man.   Of course.
Kraft (*to* Jem).
  What says the doctor, Jem ?   Will he recover?
Jem.   I thinks he thinks he will.
Kraft (*to* Madam Cecil.)
                              We're safe, at least.
  He's lived now long enough—for that.
Madam C. (*aside*).   Yet I
  Could almost pray to know that he were dead !
Cecil (*in bewilderment, starting suddenly, and sitting
     up in the bed*).
  And did you think I wished to be alive ?

CURTAIN.

ACT THIRD.

An interval of two years is supposed to elapse between the occurrences in Acts Second and Third.

SCENE FIRST : *A room in the house of* FREEMAN, *who has married* CELIA, *and is living with her in a Northern " Border " State. Near the center of the room, set with dishes for a meal, is a table. Bread and a pitcher of milk have already been placed on it. Three or four chairs are near the table. At the Left is a closet, and about the room other articles of furniture. Backing, a wall containing a window or door, etc. Entrances by doors at the Right and Left near the Front.*

The curtain rising discloses JEM *with overcoat and hat on, standing in front of the table.*

JEM (*to himself*).
De station am a mile off.   Whah's de dahky
Dat wouldn't get hungry 'fore he got dat fah ?
(*taking bread from table and putting it in his pocket.*)
Dey wouldn't want to see me stahve ; not dey !
Naw dwy up, no !
         (*taking up milk pitcher, and looking at it.*)
                Why, 'sakes alive ! dah's massa—
And what's he call me calf faw ?

(pouring out a tumbler-full of milk, drinking it,
then hiding the tumbler in the closet.)

                Dat am good.
Dis dahky's glad dat Massa Cecil's comin'.
But Massa Cecil,—wondeh how he'll take
To seein' dat Miss Cecil, Missus Fweeman.
It 'peahed as how he liked dat ah young gal.
And, when ole' Missus Cecil, she got out
And mawwied Massa Kwaft, why, me and Milly,
We 'spected Massa Cecil 'd like to get
As fuh de oder way wid his Miss Celia.—
But Massa Fweeman 's got her, got her tight.

*Enter—Left—*FREEMAN *and* CELIA, *the latter with*
tray containing more dishes for table.

FREEMAN (*to* JEM).
    It's time to go, Jem.
JEM.   Go?—I's goin',—gone!
          *Exit—Right—*JEM.
CELIA (*arranging the dishes on the table, and suspi-*
    ciously examining the bread-plate and milk-
    pitcher, while shaking her head at the departing
    JEM).
Faith's looking well?
FREEMAN (*seating himself in one of the chairs, and*
    taking a newspaper from his pocket and unfold-
    ing it).
             Much as she did of old,
But paler—that is, till she chanced to see me.
CELIA.   And then?

FREEMAN.   She flushed.

CELIA.   It needed but a spark
To kindle the old fire.

FREEMAN.   In her?—or me?—
I saw no light.   I only thought of ashes.

CELIA.   I know her nun's veil seemed a shroud to
you.

FREEMAN.   Your white one, Celia, when I married
you,
Seemed like an angel's.   Now that it's been
dropped,
I'm sure it was.

CELIA.   I thank you.   Yet, at times,
I fear 'twas pity led you to propose.

FREEMAN.   Was it your pity led you to accept?

CELIA.   You know you thought that I had closed
the door
To every other suitor by my act
In closing it on all except us two
When we were nursing Cecil.

FREEMAN.   And you know
You thought that I had closed the door on Faith,
Because of that which Father Hycher said.
But—nonsense!—what if pity were a motive?

CELIA.   Pity is but a sadder kind of love—

FREEMAN.   No love at all.   But as a motive to
it—
A door to open,—why complain of it,
If only opening where we wish to go?

(CELIA, *having ended arranging the things on the
    table, stands back looking at it*).
  And all is ready—is it ?—for our guest?
CELIA.   To think that Cecil should be here, and
    well !
FREEMAN.   And such a note as his too!   Why, a
    boy,
  A boy in love, could not more gracefully
  Let tumble forth from his embarrassed lips
  The whole sweet contents of his blushing cheeks,
  Than he did, pelting, helter-skelter, out
  Those metaphors at us, to vent his joy
  In welcoming our own !
CELIA.   'Twas strange he felt so !
FREEMAN.   Why, no; I'm worthy of you ; you of
    me ;
  And both of us of Cecil's interest.
  He knows how we two nursed him.   Now, at last,
  His voyage at an end, his health restored,
  It ought to give him joy, and pride as well,
  To learn how we, through love for him, at first,
  Have come to love each other.   Every soul
  Is proudest of the good itself has fathered.
CELIA.   Of course ; and Cecil has so kind a heart !
  But I must go, and get the breakfast ready.
FREEMAN (*rising and taking* CELIA'S *hand*).
  But, first, my Celia, let me break my fast.
                (*kisses her.*)
  One kiss of yours could make the thrilling lips

Go fluttering all day long like Cupid's wings
To bear sweet words of love to all they meet.

*Exit—Left—*CELIA.

(FREEMAN's *eyes follow her as she disappears.*)
I told no lie. She lights my life with love.
But, oh, had she been Faith, 'twere filled with
    bliss !—
Poor Celia, she shall never learn the truth.
She thinks my nature water. I did once :
If any face looked love upon its depths,
I thought they might be filled with that alone.
But, ah, my heart's a photographer's glass
Whereon the image once impressed remains ;
And Celia's face is always framed in Faith's.
I fear 'tis for the frame, I love the picture.

(*looking out of the back window nearest the Right.*)
Why, Cecil here already ?—must be he—

(FREEMAN *opens the door at the Right.*)

*Enter—Right—*CECIL *followed by* JEM. *Both*
    wear out-door costumes, CECIL *an over-*
    coat. He also carries a cane and limps.
    As he enters, he and FREEMAN *shake*
    hands.

A hearty welcome, friend ! I saw you coming.
How well you look ! You are well too, not so ?

CECIL (*removing his hat, which* JEM *takes*).
    Oh, yes.

FREEMAN (*noticing that* CECIL *limps*).
    Lame yet ?—

CECIL. Shall always be. One foot
Was caught inside the grave. I pulled away;
But drag the foot-stone.
FREEMAN (*helping* CECIL *take off his overcoat*).
Not the head-stone though!
CECIL. I hope not.
FREEMAN (*handing* CECIL'S *overcoat to* JEM, *who
takes it in addition to the hat*).
Here, Jem, take these out with you.
(FREEMAN *turns to get a chair for* CECIL.)
JEM (*aside, as he stands near the Left Entrance*).
I'd like to see what Massa Cecil 'll do
When he finds out Miss Celia's Missus Fwee-
man.
I knows, from what he say, dat he don't 'spect it.
*Exit—Right—*JEM.
FREEMAN (*placing a chair behind* CECIL).
Sit here.
CECIL (*sitting in the chair and looking around the
room*).
I thank you.—What a pleasant home!
You've heard, have you, of late, about my wife?
FREEMAN. Not since she married Kraft. 'Twas
mean in her.
CECIL. Oh no; not that!
FREEMAN (*sitting in chair*).
But getting her divorce
Was so unjust!

CECIL. Kraft managed it, of course.
I had deserted her.

FREEMAN. You could not help it.

CECIL. No; thanks to her—and heaven! But let
that rest.
When one has seemed to sleep the sleep of death—
You know I thought me dead—'tis not so sad,
On waking, to begin one's life anew.

FREEMAN. And we too thought you dead.

CECIL. I acted so?

FREEMAN. You acted not at all. You did not
stir.

CECIL. No wonder! Had you seen what I saw
then,
Your senses would have been as hushed as mine.

FREEMAN. What was it?

CECIL. I scarce know—a vision—dream—
Perhaps a trance.—Some day I'll tell you it.

FREEMAN. If dreams came true, a man might prize
them more.

CECIL. At times, they do come true. Mine will.
The power
That handles Kraft can make that devil spin
Like potter's clay to work out his designs.
It all was prophesied.

FREEMAN. Was prophesied?

CECIL. Yes,—in my vision,—all about—your marriage.

FREEMAN. My marriage?

CECIL.   Yes, and then such joy for me !—
I know 'tis coming.

FREEMAN.   So ?—I envy you.

CECIL. I thought me dead. I woke and all was
    life.
Above, I saw the stars ; far east, the dawn.
If earth rolls on, it yet will bring full day.

FREEMAN. And bright may heaven make it !

CECIL.   That it will.
Earth is a field where hidden treasure lies.
All search it, and their searching wakes their
    thoughts,
And draws out their desires, and aims their acts.
At last, they look and live for that alone
Which lures beneath appearances. Few find it.
The few that do, find that which makes the
    world
Worth living in, and worth yon circling dome,
The crown God made it, jeweled with his stars.

FREEMAN. And you have found it ?

CECIL.   Freeman, yes, I have ;
And know why sometimes earth seems holy
    ground,
And those that tread it Godlike. 'Tis the face
Behind the veil that then shines dimly through
    it.
But wait. I must not tell you. In our souls,
Far down within, are depths like sunken seas,
So dark !—yet only when concealed from light

And from the face of love they else might image.
Mine hold such. You should know of these, to know
My coming joy; yet need not. Soon you'll guess it.

FREEMAN. Your mood alone can make one guess enough
To offer his congratulations now.

(FREEMAN *rises. So does* CECIL, *and they shake hands.*)
'Tis time though that your coming were an-
.nounced.
There's one here will be but too glad to see you.

*Exit—Left—*FREEMAN.

CECIL (*reseating himself*).
How kind his welcome is ! 'Tis worth some loss
To know we own some friends.—And Faith, too, Faith,—
She too, he says, will be so glad to see me.
I always liked her; and I always knew
The two were lovers, and they knew I knew it.
This must have been the reason why his note
Made such a mere brief mention of his mar-
riage ;
As if, forsooth, I knew the news already.
I thought I must have missed one letter from him.
But no ; what need of sending me her name !—
Who could she be but Faith !—This very room

Seems like her.   There's no setting that becomes
A jewel of a woman like a home,—
A loving home like this.   Thank God, some
    souls
Need not to die before they find their mates.
And I shall not.—Ah, when that shot was fired
That almost freed my soul, you, Celia, thought
I sank unconscious.   No, no ; not before
Heaven let me hear this much : " He's dead for
    me,
The only man I ever loved is dead ! "
Then came my dream.—But you, you are so
    young,—
May deem yourself too young for me !   Yet
    there's
No risk of losing you.   I'll show my spirit ;
And with that spirit which is one with mine,
You'll recognize it.   Then I'll thank my stars
For cloud and storm and flash that struck me
    down,
And heaven in life that followed death in life.
> *Enter—Right Second Entrance—*CELIA.
> (*She carries another dish for table.   As she en-
>   ters, before she is where she can speak to
>   *CECIL, *he says, aside.*)
What ?—Celia here ?   And I was never told it ?—
> (*rising to greet her.*)
Why, Freeman said that I should find a friend.
I have—the friend to whom I owe my life.

CELIA (*placing the dish on table, and shaking hands with him*).

Had it been lost, it would have been for me.

CECIL. Now that 'tis saved, let it be saved for you.

CELIA. For me and all who love you.

CECIL (*aside*). Ah, who love!

(*to* CELIA.)

I would that I could always stay with you.

CELIA. You would not go away?

CECIL. What, would you wish me
To make my home with you?

CELIA. Of course.—Why not?

CECIL. But I must work.

CELIA. And one can practice law
In any place?

CECIL (*taking her hand*).
Shall I begin it here?

CELIA. Begin and keep on too.

CECIL. I think I wlll.

CELIA. 'Twould please us so!

CECIL. And could you ever think
That I could feel at home away from you?

CELIA. How kind in you to say that!—Then you'll live
Right here with me and Freeman?

CECIL. You and Freeman?

CELIA. Why, certainly!—He'll want it, too.

CECIL. I see.—
You two together saved my life, of course.

CELIA. Of course we saved it, if it could be saved.

CECIL. And so you live with him?

CELIA.   Yes, that's the reason.—
It was our mutual interest in you.

*Enter—Left—*FREEMAN.

(*Just as he enters,* CELIA, *bowing to* CECIL *and gesturing toward the table, indicates that she must prepare for the meal, and moves toward the Left.*)

FREEMAN (*holding newspaper in hand, and bringing it to* CECIL).

Oh, here's the morning paper! Would you like it?

*Exit—Left—*CELIA.

(CECIL *bows, takes paper from* FREEMAN, *and sits in chair.* FREEMAN *returns to closet near Left, and, while carrying on the following conversation, finds there a small bottle, which, when presently he leaves the room, he takes with him.*)

CECIL. She says that I'm to live with you and her.

FREEMAN. Yes, we had hoped so.

CECIL (*looking at* CELIA'S *retreating form*).

                              Freeman, this is bliss!

FREEMAN. Yes, we are very happy.

CECIL.   That we are!—
Men do not often wed their own ideals.

FREEMAN. I know. I've thought the whole thing
    through ; and yet,
Without that, life can have some brightness left.
CECIL. Without that?—You mistake my meaning,
    Freeman.
I'm not to live without that. No, indeed !
She loves me, Freeman. There's no doubt of it.
FREEMAN. Who ?
CECIL.   Celia !
FREEMAN.   Celia ?
CECIL.   Celia, yes.—Why not?
FREEMAN. You mean ?—
CECIL.   Oh, yes, you think that she's too young !
But, Freeman, love is of th' eternities, and knows
No youth, nor age. 'Tis like the air of heaven
That tosses in its play the dangling fringe
Athrill with grace about our outward guise,
And runs its unseen fingers through our hair,
And brushes to a glow our flushing cheeks,
But has more serious lasting moods than these.
It is the substance of the breath we breathe
That keeps the blood fresh, and the heart in
    motion ;
And, e'en when these give out, it still is there
To buoy us up and bear on high the spirit.
FREEMAN. Oh, yes !—but Celia ?—
CECIL.   Celia is my love.
FREEMAN. Your love, eh?—Has she told you
    that ?

CECIL.   She has.

FREEMAN.   Told you she loves you?

CECIL.   Is it past belief?

FREEMAN.   Well—yes—I think it is.

CECIL.   Oh, you know not

What's in a woman's heart!

(CECIL *looks down at his paper, as if reading.*)

FREEMAN (*aside*).

                                    It may be not.

I purpose to find out, though.—Is he mad?
Am I mad?—My sole proof that I am not,
Lies in my thinking that I may be so.—
I'll cultivate this thinking and keep sane;
And if it be a cool head takes the trick,
I'll find what trick is here.

(FREEMAN *opens door at the Left.*)

*Enter—Left—*CELIA.

(*She carries something else for the table.*)

CECIL (*seeing* CELIA *coming*).

                                    Here she comes.—

She'll tell you it herself.

CELIA (*placing what she brings on the table, then
    busying herself with arranging things on it*).

                                    I'm coming now,

To stay with you awhile.

CECIL (*to* CELIA).

                                    To be with those

Who really love one, is a new delight.
You said you loved me, Celia.

CELIA.   Why, of course—
Just as I always have, and always must.
Of course I do.

*Exit—Left—*FREEMAN, *lifting his hands in a be-*
wildered way.

CECIL (*aside, as* CELIA *turns away for something*).
                    Of course !
          (*then noticing that* FREEMAN *had left.*)
                    Why, there.   He's gone.—
Humph !   Who could wonder that he thinks it
    strange.
I wonder Celia fails to think so too.
It proves how well our natures mate each other.
                    (*to* CELIA.)
Look—Freeman's left us, Celia.—Have a care.
To love too much may make him envious ;
And chewing on the cud of jealousy
Is not a pleasant practice for one's friends.
For though you give them naught to work upon,
So much the more the grinders work away
And grind themselves the sharper,—ay, and grind
The words that pass them too—made sharp as
    arrows
To pierce the soul they hit.
CELIA.   No fear of him !—
We both of us love you.
CECIL.   I'll punish him !
When he comes in, I'll send him after Faith.
CELIA.   No ; you must not do that.
    9

CECIL.   Oh, yes, I shall.

CELIA (*taking a seat on the opposite side of the table from him*).

   You would not dare.—

CECIL.   Not dare ?—Ha, ha, ha, ha !

CELIA.   No, no ; I beg you not to——

CECIL.   Nonsense, Celia !

CELIA.   You must not.

CECIL.   Must not ?—And you really mean it ?—
   Oh, well, if you're in earnest, I will not.
   But, bless me, if I see the reason why.

CELIA.   He loves Faith.

CECIL.   Yes ; and where would be my joke,
   Unless he loved her ?

CELIA.   There was so much love,
   I sometimes think that he is sad about it.

CECIL.   What ? what ?—not happy in his married
   life ?

CELIA.   Oh, one could not say that.   He's very
   kind.

CECIL.   Yes, yes ?—and she ?—is she not kind to
   him ?

CELIA.   Who?   Faith ?

CECIL.   Yes, Faith.

CELIA.   He never hears from her.

CECIL.   What ?—Are they separated ?

CELIA.   Separated !
   She went—you hadn't heard it ?—to a convent.

CECIL. She did ?—Poor Freeman !—When was that ?

CELIA. Last year.

CECIL (*in a perplexed way*).

But when was Freeman married ?

CELIA. Why, last March.—

He wrote you all about it.

CECIL (*startled*).

No ; not all,—

Not half a page.

CELIA (*surprised*).

Why, twenty pages, friend !—

We both wrote twenty ; and you never got them ?

CECIL. Why, no ; you see I hadn't heard of
Faith—

(*hesitatingly.*)

And you now—you are living with him here ?

CELIA. Yes, living !—Did you think that we were
boarding ?

CECIL (*aside*).

What horror haunts me ?—But I must not show
it.

(*slowly, and struggling to conceal emotion.*)

You know—it seems—so strange—when — he
loved Faith.

CELIA. What ?—That he married me ? —He told
me all ;

But Faith seemed dead.

CECIL (*controlling himself*).

And he's a kind man, Celia ?

CELIA. Yes, very kind.

16

CECIL.   Forgive me, will you, Celia ?
You see that I have always loved you, Celia,—
Just as a father loves a child, you know ;
And if my love be anxious for you, Celia,
            *Enter—Left—*FREEMAN.
        (*He is not observed by* CECIL *or* CELIA. *He re-
        places in the closet the little bottle taken
        from it, when on the stage the previous
        time. While doing so, he evidently hears
        the following conversation.*)
You will not think it strange ?
CELIA.   There's not a throb
In all my heart, but you've a right to know it.
CECIL.   Your heart is satisfied ?
CELIA.   Yes, yes, my love
Is deep and true.   No wife could love one more.
            *Exit—Left—*FREEMAN.
CECIL.   Then you have two friends,—him and me.
      You stand
Between us.
CELIA (*rising*).   I must go now.
CECIL (*rising*).   Yes, my daughter !
            *Exit—Left—*CELIA.
(*standing, and looking after her retreating form*).
So close the clouds of heaven upon my dream !—
Not God,—the devil—he, he rules the world !—
If so, I'll rule it with him.—But no, no !—
Oh, what a universe of agencies
Are centered in one life that may be both

The God and devil of the soul it loves !
Yet wits were given one to outwit the world.
If Celia be what I have dreamed she is,
The world must work its work upon her will
Without one touch of mine, or hint, or sigh,
To make her life more tempted or less true.—
Oh, cursed world, in which forswearing love
Is our best proof that we would foster it !
But wait !—What moves me ?—Am I but a fool
Controlled by dreams ?—No, no ; I had a
   dream ;
But this, at least, is none,—that each who aids
An angel upward for himself prepares
Angelic friendship ; and if there be spheres
Where spirit can reveal itself to spirit,
And sympathy be sovereign, there must be
One soul supremely loved. 'Twas no mere
   dream.
High, knightly chivalry whose love protects,
Thy knightly honor *is* the sacred thing
Of which thy pride is conscious. But—oh
   God !—
To be just on the threshold of all bliss :
And fail.—Fail ?—No. Let Freeman have her
   now
A few brief years.—I'll dream with her forever.
             *Enter—Right—*JEM.
Ah, what is that?—Who's there ?—Well, Jem,
   what now ?

JEM. Some white folks heah as wants to speak wid
you.

CECIL (*in surprise*).

With me ?—I've no objection.—Bid them enter.

Enter—Right—as JEM *holds open door,* THREE
GENTLEMEN. *They wear overcoats and
hold their hats in their hands.* CECIL *ex-
changes bows with them, and motions toward the chairs.*

You'll sit, not so ?

FIRST GENTLEMAN. No, thanks. We have no time.

Our party's first convention meets to-morrow.

The news is ominous. We may have war.

We came as a committee to request

To hear from you.

CECIL. 　　　　　To hear from me ?—and why ?

FIRST GENT. You've suffered from the wrongs of
slavery

That we oppose.

CECIL. 　　　But I'm a stranger here.

FIRST GENT. Good reputation is to good men
what

Fine fragrance is to flowers. Its charms for sense

Are scented by imagination too,

Which will not rest till eyes have seen their
source.

CECIL. You do me too much honor.

FIRST GENT. 　　　　　　　　Honor us ;

And let us see and hear you.

CECIL. If my words——

FIRST GENT. The words of men whose deeds have
proved them true
Are also true.

CECIL. Thanks. If you think them so,
They may at least command your interest.
And he whose words can hold the world to
thought
Has heaven's own warrant that he should be
heard.
Yes ; I will come.

FIRST GENT. Thanks.

SECOND GENT AND THIRD. Thanks.

> (*All move toward Left Second Entrance. JEM
> who is nearest it opens door there. CECIL
> and GENTS exchange bows.*)

CECIL. I'll see you out.

*Exeunt—Right—*THREE GENTS, CECIL *and* JEM.

———

SCENE SECOND : *An open field or village green. Backing in the distance, village houses, and beyond them
hill scenery. Extending diagonally across stage
from the place of the Right Third Entrance toward
that of the Back Center, a cottage fronted by a porch,
the latter being a platform elevated a foot or two
above the rest of the stage. At the Left of the stage
are trees and a tent, apparently one of a soldiers'
encampment beyond it.*

ENTRANCES : *Right Second between trees, Right*

Upper from a door opening from the cottage on to the porch; Back Center from behind the cottage; Left Second, Third and Upper, from behind trees, or the tent.

As the curtain rises, SOLDIERS *and* POPULACE *are seen grouped at the Left.*

(*They sing as follows :*)

The trumpet calls to action
  Through all the threatened land
No more is heard of faction.
  The time has come to band.
    What soul can see
The state in fear and fail to be
Beneath the flag, enrolled with all
  That heed the trumpet's call?
      No patriot he, whose soul can see
      The state in fear and fail to be
      Beneath the flag, enrolled with all
      That heed the trumpet's call.

The best of men are brothers.
  The worst can be a foe ;
And not for self but others,
  True men to battle go.
    No longer meek,
Where wrong is strong and right is weak,
Or aught has brought the base to band,—
  They're there to lend a hand.
      No true man he, whose soul can see
      The state in fear, and fail to be
      Beneath the flag, enrolled with all
      That heed the trumpet's call.

Who, think you, live in story
That live for self alone?
Who care to swell his glory
That cares not for their own?
In every strife
That stirs the pulse to nobler life,
'Tis he that has the thrilling heart
Who plays the thrilling part.
No hero he, whose soul can see
The state in fear, and fail to be
Beneath the flag, enrolled with all
That heed the trumpet's call.

*Exeunt—Left—*SOLDIERS *and* POPULACE.
*Enter—Back Center—*CECIL, *in out-door costume.*
*Enter—Right Second—*FAITH, *dressed as a nun.*
CECIL (*to himself*).

These clouds of war break like a thunder-clap
Amid clear skies of summer; but will bring
Our plant of freedom to a finer fruitage.
     (*suddenly observing* FAITH.)
Faith Hycher?
FAITH.   Yes—on business.
CECIL.   With me?
FAITH.   Old friends of ours are here—have interest
In land near by us. Being of the south
They came to place it where they might not lose it.
They've been arrested. People deem them spies.
CECIL. Who are they?
FAITH.   Why, my mother, Father Hycher,
Lowe, Blaver, Kraft——

CECIL. His wife too ?

FAITH. Yes.

CECIL. Humph, humph !

FAITH. Their holdings were not small. The time
was short.

All came here who might need to sign their papers.

CECIL. And what can I do ?

FAITH. Say you know them—you
And Freeman.

CECIL. You ve seen Freeman, then ?

FAITH (*hesitating*). No—I——

CECIL (*kindly*).

I understand you, Faith.

FAITH. 'Twas not his fault :
I was deceived.

CECIL. By whom ?

FAITH. By Father Hycher.

CECIL. And yet you wish to help him now ?

FAITH. I do.

CECIL. As I should help the Krafts ?—We'll work
together.

Faith, you and I have loved supremely,—yet
Our love has loved another.—Could this be
Of that form which we walked with in our
dreams ?

FAITH. Why——

CECIL. Did you ever think that all our dreams
Are in ourselves ; and this form too may be there ?
They say that human brains, ay, all our frames

Are doubled.—If so, why?—For use?—then
　whose?—
Who is it twins existence with us here?
Can it be our own real, live, better self
Which under consciousness we vaguely feel
Dreams while we wake and wakes the while we
　dream,
Recalls what we forget, incites, and is
Less form than spirit, but, because a spirit,
Heaven's representative, our guardian, guide,
And all that tells of God? You know all praise
The men dependent only on themselves.
Yet why?—Is it so noble to be free
From love, or wish for love? Or own these men
A subtle consciousness of nobler love
Which, in the spirit-life, is all in all?
Know they that earthly forms which seem divine
But image that within which is divine?—
You think you wedded to the church.—I'm not.
Yet, Faith, the bonds that bind us may not
　differ.—
I'll help your friends. When needed, call upon me.
FAITH. You're kind.
Exit—Right—after exchanging bows with CECIL,
　　　　FAITH.
CECIL (*to himself, as he stands near this Entrance,
　and close to the porch*).
　　　　For her, for me, for all whose paths
Of honor and of sympathy divide,

One choice alone remains—to dwell content
With loneliness, and one's ideal, and God.

*Enter—Right Upper—coming suddenly from the
cottage on to the porch,* CELIA.

CELIA (*to* CECIL).

Save, save my husband !

CECIL.   Save from what ?

CELIA.   From death,
From certain death.

CECIL.   To march to war is not
To march to certain death.

CELIA.   My throbbing heart
Would spend its blood in blushes for my shame
Till it forgot to give my being life,
If, by a single sigh, I durst keep back
One soldier from the ranks of this just war.

CECIL.   What mean you, then ?

CELIA.   That he has volunteered
To act as spy, and in the very town
Where he has lived, is known, and hated too.
He can but be detected.

CECIL.   You are right.
I see him coming.

(*pointing to the Left.*—CELIA *looks at him, in-
quiringly.*)
You had better leave us.

*Exit—Right Upper—*CELIA.

*Enter—Left Second—*FREEMAN, *dressed as an officer.*
(*to* FREEMAN).

Your wife says you have volunteered to act
As spy, where you are sure to meet with death.
FREEMAN. I may succeed.
CECIL. You scarce can hope to do so.
FREEMAN (*with assumed indifference*).
And what if not?
CECIL. Then you are not the man
To trust on such a mission.
FREEMAN. Not?—How so?
CECIL. No man, if wise, will waive from what he plans
The prospect of success. If you attempt it,
I'll find a way to stop it.
FREEMAN. You're officious.
CECIL. One needs to be at times; and now your life
And Celia's happiness are both at stake.
FREEMAN. Not Celia's happiness.
CECIL. What do you mean?
FREEMAN. I mean, since men have talked so much against
Our owning blacks, the time is coming fast
For some to talk against our owning whites.
CECIL. And what suggested this?
FREEMAN. You know—you know.
We've both seen men and women treat their peers—
In wedlock, yes, but also out of it—
As if they owned them; and society

Approved, enforced their course.   Mere selfish-
   ness
Has been enthroned so long in men's affairs,
That naught seems worthy of respect to some
Of which it only is not king and guide.

CECIL.   And, pray, too, what of that ?

FREEMAN.   If Celia find
   More joy in your society than mine,
Then let her find it.   Did I marry her
To limit her delights ?

CECIL.   Why, Freeman, friend,
   Look here at me—You are an upright man,
     (*placing his hand on* FREEMAN'S *shoulder.*)
And so am I.   Upon my soul, I hoped
You had forgotten, or not understood
The words I used.   But, ere I knew you married,
Was it—with all that she and I had been—
So strange that I should have—those—whims of
   mine ?

FREEMAN.   She told you that she loved you.

CECIL.   Yes, she did :
   But as a daughter.
       (FREEMAN *looks incredulous.*)
          I am not the man
You should distrust.

FREEMAN.   Who knows what men can be,
   Till pierced where they are tenderest !   'Twas the
     fleet
Achilles could be wounded in the heel ;

And some have heads, and some have hearts to
 hurt.
CECIL.   I say she said she loved me as a daughter.
 I quote her very words.
FREEMAN.   She said no more ?
CECIL.   When speaking of her love, she said no
 more.
 She gave no slightest hint that meant not that.
FREEMAN.   Yet you love her ?
CECIL.   In the degree I do,
 I'll guard her honor as I would mine own ;
 And guard her love too.   She has told me all.
 She loves you as a true and faithful wife.
 So let me save you for her.   Be no spy,
 But soldier, captain, general,—who knows
 What fortune may await the tide of war !
FREEMAN.   And you ?
CECIL.   Why, Freeman, I'm no man to play
 A second fiddle to your tune of love—
 With instrument all broke beyond repair,
 Make discord of the music of your life.
 I promise you to leave here.
FREEMAN.   Leave your home ?—
 You have no other.
CECIL.   Some will open for me.
            (*pointing toward the tent.*)
 There were one here, did my infirmities
 Not keep me from the army.
            (*Shouts are heard at the Left.*)
 8

Enter—Left—A guard of Soldiers *headed by*
an Officer, *and conducting* Blaver *and*
Miss Primwood—*now* Madam Blaver
—Lowe *and* Madam Lowe, Father Hy-
cher, Kraft *and* Madam Cecil—*now*
Madam Kraft—Father Hycher *and*
Widow Hycher, *attended by* Faith.
Populace *follow.*

Freeman (*in evident astonishment*).

Who are they?

Cecil.   I think you know them.

Freeman (*noticing* Father Hycher).

Father Hycher?—I'll
Get even with him.

Cecil.   No; there's no such thing
As getting even with a low-lived soul,
Without degrading one's own self.

(*to the* Officer.)

And what
Of these?

Officer.   They're spies.

Other People.   To shoot.

Others.   They've land, as well,
To confiscate.

Officer (*to* Cecil).   They tell us that you know
them.

Cecil.   Why, yes; and Freeman too.—Ah, Madam
Blaver!

(Cecil *and* Freeman *shake hands with* Miss

PRIMWOOD—*now* MADAM BLAVER—*with*
MADAM LOWE, WIDOW HYCHER, LOWE
and BLAVER, *but not with the others.*
CECIL *continues to the* OFFICER, *gesturing toward the ladies, including* MADAM
CECIL—*now* MADAM KRAFT.)
Our war is not with ladies, I believe?
(*The* OFFICER *apparently agrees with him.*)

FATHER HYCHER.   I am a clergyman.
CECIL.   'Tis true; and we?—
(*looking for assent to* FREEMAN.)
FREEMAN. Of course, we have no strife here with
    religion.
LOWE.   I am a friend.
CECIL.   He is.
LOWE.   With me the chief
Consideration is religion.
BLAVER.   And I
A prohibitionist.   Our pleas were all
Based on religious grounds.
OFFICER.   And what of that?
FREEMAN (*laughing*).   You fail to catch its bear·
    ing?—When we make
Them take an oath of loyalty, they'll keep it.
(*The prisoners make startled signs of dissent.*)
CECIL. There's this' much to be said too: as a
    rule
The friends are on our side; and are not fighters.
So too with prohibitionists.
10

FREEMAN (*to* CECIL, *in a laughing way*).

       For once,
 Religion, friend, has helped them in their
  practice.

OFFICER (*taking* KRAFT *roughly by the shoulder*).
 But here's a different case.

CECIL.   I grant it, yes.

OFFICER. We know him, and his party.

MADAM CECIL-KRAFT (*to* CECIL). Could I speak
 A moment with you?

CECIL.   Oh, yes, if it please you.

(CECIL *and* MADAM CECIL-KRAFT, *walk to one side.*)

MADAM C. You know my father died.

CECIL (*nodding toward* KRAFT). Before you married?

    (MADAM C. *nods in assent.*)
 A happy man!

MADAM C.   He left a fortune to me.
 'Tis in this land here.

CECIL.   And in Kraft's name?

MADAM C.   Yes.
   (*hesitatingly, after pausing a moment.*)
 There was an informality——

CECIL.   In what?

MADAM C. My marriage.

CECIL.   I should think so!—What of that?

MADAM C. Why, I would deed you half my
 ownings here,
 Could it——

CECIL.   Be set aside by me ?

MADAM C.   With you—
  Your help.

CECIL.   No, thank you—not for all you own.

MADAM C.   And you would have me lose it, would
    you ?

CECIL.   You
  Forget my losses.

MADAM C. (*pretending to misunderstand him, and to
    relent toward him*).
                    And you really miss me ?

CECIL.   That's   not   worth   speaking   of — but
    Kraft ?

MADAM C. (*disparagingly*).   Oh, he !—

CECIL.   He treats you as you might have judged
    from Celia ?

MADAM C. (*sarcastically*).
  And Celia treats you as you might have judged—

CECIL.   From other women ? —No ; all cooing doves
  Have not one color——

MADAM C.   Only cawing crows.

CECIL.   You know some think it sin to shoot at
    crows.

MADAM C.   And manly sportsmen never   aim   at
    doves.

CECIL.   When things are very far removed from us,
  It is excusable if we mistake them.

KRAFT (*coming forward, followed by* FREEMAN).
  But surely you will help us ?

CECIL.   Surely ?—why ?
          (*motioning toward* MADAM C.).
  You have relieved me here, and therefore think
  That one good turn deserves another ?
KRAFT.   But
  You know I'm not a spy.
CECIL.   How do I know it ?
KRAFT.   My character——
CECIL.   What character ?—You think
  My character is one to forge a lie
  To save a man like you ?
KRAFT.   What—you would not ?
MADAM C.   Why, all our property is here !
KRAFT.   And you
  Would have me shot ?
CECIL (*to* FREEMAN).
                    There's an idea there.—
  Might do it kindly—in a better cause
  Than his past deeds deserve.
FREEMAN.   I see.
              (*to the* SOLDIERS.)
                    Say, friends,
  We're here to save the lands of loyal men.
  All loyal men about us are enlisting.
  If Kraft has loyalty, he'll do the same.
      (*The* SOLDIERS *make signs of approval.*)
              (*to* KRAFT.)
  What say you ?

KRAFT (*hesitatingly*).
>   Had I—a—commission——

FREEMAN.   That
>   Would prove the one who gave it you a fool.

CECIL (*to* KRAFT, *putting his hand on* FREEMAN'S
>   *shoulder*).
>   Places of trust are only for the trusted ;
>   And high commissions but for men with mis-
>   sions.
>   What say you—prison or private ?—Make your
>   choice.

KRAFT (*abjectly*).
>   Why, if I must——

CECIL.   'Tis well to learn you must.
>   *Enter—Left—hurriedly,* TWO GENTLEMEN.
>   (*Commotion among the* POPULACE *near them and fol-
>   lowing them.*)

POPULACE.   Hurrah !
>   *Enter—Right Upper—evidently attracted by
>   the commotion,* CELIA, *followed by* JEM
>   *and* MILLY, *and stand on the porch.*

FIRST GENTLEMAN (*to* CECIL).   They've nominated
>   you.

CECIL.   For what ?

FIRST GENT.   For representative at Washington.

SECOND GENT. (*shaking hands with* CECIL).
>   And I congratulate the district too.

CECIL.   But I'm a stranger.

FIRST GENT.   No, your record's known.

SECOND GENT.   The only home you have now must
    be here ;
For here they brought and nursed you, when so
    ill.
FIRST GENT.   And when the factions could not else
    agree,
They all could join on you.
PEOPLE.   Hurrah ! hurrah !
SECOND GENT.   And nomination here is sure elec-
    tion.
PEOPLE.   Hurrah ! hurrah ! hurrah !   A speech ! a
    speech !
CECIL (*ascending the porch, where he stands with*
    CELIA *at his Right*).
This is no time for words or peaceful work ;
But one whose forced infirmities prevent
His bearing arms and marching to the front,
May choose the course that you commend to him.
(*Cheers from the crowd.*   CECIL *gestures toward the*
    SOLDIERS.)
But do not think you only move to war ;
Or deem that I stay here to dwell in peace.
To men whose purposes, like ours, are pledged
To work out high designs, all life on earth
Is girt with warfare, where the light of heaven
That brings each new day's liberty and truth
Contends with darkness, and there is no peace.
Our very bodies are but phantoms formed
Of that same darkness that we must oppose ;

So we must fight, if nothing else, ourselves.
Ay, whether we may march our frames to greet
The cannon's mouth, or duty's commoner call,
Go where death threatens soon, or seems to
    tarry,
One destiny, at last, awaits us all :
Upon life's little stage the play will close,
The curtain drop, and leave the actor dead.
Yet, soldiers, what care you, or what care I ?—
The souls that fight for truth, beyond these
    scenes,
Find life that does not end in tragedy ;
For all our world is but a theater
Outside whose walls, where shine the stars of
    heaven,
The actors with their rôles and robes laid by
May all meet smiling in the open air.
And now—to play our several parts—

(*bowing to those before him, then turning to* CELIA *and
taking her hand.*)
                      Farewell.
(*Blast of bugles, as the* SOLDIERS *fall into line, with*
KRAFT *well guarded.*)

CURTAIN.

END.

From the press of the Arena Publishing Company.

Two Dramas for the Library Corner.

Price, cloth, $1.25.

Walter Warren

COLUMBUS THE DISCOVERER. A Drama.

Printed on beautiful paper, wide margins, and richly bound.

Walter Warren has struck boldly into the most ambitious field of poetical literature, and he has produced three dramas which will obtain a wide reading among people who read and study the best in contemporary literature.

The story of Columbus has been the subject of many a novel during the past two or three years, and now it is brought again before the public in the form of a spirited drama in five acts. Mr. Walter Warren makes a psychologic rather than historic — though not unhistoric — study of the character of Columbus, as manifested and developed in connection with his experiences before, during and after his discovery of America. In dramatizing the story in this fashion, one gains a better insight into the personality of Columbus than is possible from the merely abstract narratives. Its many parts are practically arranged for amateur theatricals. — *The Boston Herald.*

Price, cloth, $1.25.

THE AZTECS.

Printed uniform with "Columbus the Discoverer," and richly bound. A fine library volume.

Mr. Walter Warren is a man evidently warm in sympathy for his kind. His play is gorgeous with the local color of Mexico in the fifteenth century, and replete with fine thoughts, which, however, he acknowledges might not have come to Aztecs, although again, he alleges they might. Its plot is a noble conception. — *The Commonwealth, Boston.*

This is a drama dating back in history to the fifteenth century, when the Aztecs in Mexico began to reach out and overrun the land and introduce the peculiar religion of the time. The leading characters are Monaska, a young Mexican of noble blood; Kootha, a crippled Teztucan; Haijo, the chief priest; Wapella, a Teztucan warrior; Waloon, a Teztucan maiden of rank; with other maidens, "Virgins of the sun." These maidens of the sun were virgins taken from their homes, educated in convents, and intended for the king's palaces and seraglios. The design of the drama is to introduce the character of the peculiar religion of this ancient race and the manners and customs of daily life. . . . There are gleams of large intelligence and civilization among the ancient Aztecs, and the reader will be interested in the story. — *Chicago Inter-Ocean, Aug. 18, 1894.*

For sale by all newsdealers, or sent postpaid by
    Arena Publishing Co., Boston, Mass.

From the press of the Arena Publishing Company.

" The Hit of the Year."

Price, paper, 50 cents; cloth, $1.25.

Helen H. Gardener

AN UNOFFICIAL PATRIOT.

Have you read Helen H. Gardener's new war story, "An Unofficial Patriot"? No? Then read what competent critics say of this remarkable historical story of the Civil War.

Chicago Times

"Helen H. Gardener has made for herself within a very few years an enviable fame for the strength and sincerity of her writing on some of the most important phases of modern social questions. Her most recent novel, now published under the title of 'An Unofficial Patriot,' is no less deserving of praise. As an artistic piece of character study this book is possessed of superior qualities. There is nothing in it to offend the traditions of an honest man, north or south. It is written with an evident knowledge of the circumstances and surroundings such as might have made the story a very fact, and, more than all, it is written with an assured sympathy for humanity and a recognition of right and wrong wherever found. As to the literary merit of the book and its strength as a character study, as has been said heretofore, it is a superior work. The study of Griffith Davenport, the clergyman, and of his true friend, 'Lengthy' Patterson, is one to win favor from every reader. There are dramatic scenes in their association that thrill and touch the heart. Davenport's two visits to President Lincoln are other scenes worthy of note for the same quality, and they show an appreciation of the feeling and motive of the president more than historical in its sympathy. Mrs. Gardener may well be proud of her success in the field of fiction."

The Literary Hit of the Season

Rockford (Ill.) Republican

"Helen Gardener's new novel, ' An Unofficial Patriot,' which is just out, will probably be the most popular and salable novel since ' Robert Elsmere.' It is by far the most finished and ambitious book yet produced by the gifted author and well deserves a permanent place in literature.

"The plot of the story itself guarantees the present sale. It is ' something new under the sun ' and strikes new sensations, new situations, new conditions. To be sure it is a war story, and war stories are old and hackneyed. But there has been no such war story as this written. It gives a situation new in fiction and tells the story of the war from a standpoint which gives the book priceless value as a sociological study and as supplemental history.   .

"The plot is very strong and is all the more so when the reader learns that it is true. The story is an absolutely true one and is almost entirely a piece of history written in form of fiction, with names and minor incidents altered."

For sale by all newsdealers, or sent postpaid by
Arena Publishing Co., Boston, Mass.

Fiction : Social, Economic and Reformative.

Price, paper, 50 *cents; cloth,* $1.25.

E. Stillman
Doubleday

JUST PLAIN FOLKS.

A novel for the industrial millions, illustrating two stupendous facts : —

1. The bounty and goodness of nature.

2. The misery resulting from unjust social conditions which enable the acquirer of wealth to degenerate in luxury and idleness, and the wealth producer to slave himself to death, haunted by an ever-present fear of starvation when not actually driven to vice or begging. It is an exceedingly interesting book, simply and affectingly told, while there is a vast deal of the philosophy of communism in the moralizing of Old Bat. All persons interested in wholesome fiction. and who also desire to understand the conditions of honest industry and society-made vice, should read this admirable story.

A story of the Struggles of Honest Industry under Present Day Conditions.

Price, paper, 50 *cents ; cloth,* $1.25.

Charles S.
Daniel

Ai : A Social Vision.

One of the most ingenious, unique and thought-provoking stories of the present generation. It is a social vision, and in many respects the most noteworthy of the many remarkable dreams called forth by the general unrest and intellectual activity of the present generation. But unlike most social dreams appearing since the famous "Utopia" of Sir Thomas More, this book has distinctive qualities which will commend it to many readers who take, as yet, little interest in the vital social problems of the hour. A quiet humor pervades the whole volume which is most delightful.

A Story of the Transformation of the Slums

The brotherhood of man and various sociological and philanthropic ideas, such as the establishment of a college settlement and the social regeneration of Old Philadelphia, are a few of the topics discussed in " Ai," a novel by Charles Daniel, who calls it " A Social Vision." It is alternately grave and gay; and the intellectual freshness reminds one constantly of Edward Everett Hale's stories, with which " Ai " has much in common. This is a clever book, and, what is much more important, one whose influence is for good. — *Public Ledger.*

From the press of the Arena Publishing Company.

The Latest Social Vision.

Price, paper, 50 cents ; cloth, $1.25.

Byron A. Brooks

EARTH REVISITED.

The New Utopia, " Earth Revisited," is the latest social vision, and in many respects the most charming work of this character which has ever appeared. In it we see the people, the state and the church under true civilization, and the new psychology is introduced in such a manner as to interest students of psychical research.

Here are a few press opinions : —

Richmond, Va. Star

" As a story, it is very interesting."

Chicago Times

" Worthy of consideration for its study of the social and other questions involved."

Review of Reviews

"The story is written in an autobiographical form and pictures the social, industrial, religious and educational America of 1992. As a work of fiction the volume embodies in a fanciful way a view expressed in the closing words : 'To live is to love and to labor. There is no death.' The style is clear and direct."

Lyman Abbott's Paper, The Outlook

"Mr. Brooks is an earnest man. He has written a religio-philosophical novel of life in the coming century. The hero of this story has lived the life of the average man and at length, when he finds himself dying, he wishes that he might have a chance to live his life over. The wish is granted and he is born again on the earth a century later. Social and scientific and religious evolution have in a hundred years contrived to make an almost irrecognizable world of it. Human nature is changed; altruism is fully realized; worship has become service of man; the struggle for wealth and social rank has ended. Mr. Brooks' book is worth reading by all sincere people, and in particular by those interested in Christian socialism and applied Christianity."

Nashville, Tenn. Banner

"If you should happen to pick up Byron A. Brooks' ' Earth Revisited ' and read the first chapter, the chances are that you would follow the story on to the end, even if you had other things on hand spoiling for your attention. Summed up, ' Earth Revisited ' is a wild though delightful story, short enough to be filled from end to end with throbbing interest and long enough to fully round off the things that are introduced."

For sale by all newsdealers, or sent postpaid by
Arena Publishing Co., Boston, Mass.

Two Novels of Absorbing Interest.

Price, paper, 50 cents ; cloth, $1.25.

Eibert Hubbard

FORBES OF HARVARD.

In "Forbes of Harvard" Mr. Elbert Hubbard has produced a work which has won the unqualified praise of all lovers of clean, wholesome and elevated fiction. Below we give some critical opinions of this most delightful work.

Syracuse Herald

"'Forbes of Harvard.' A delicate and artistic piece of work, full of high-toned sentiment, good-natured and finely shaded character drawing."

Boston Times

"The book has a flavor of Concord, and the influence of Emerson, the Alcotts and Thoreau is felt throughout it. It is philosophical, moral, religious and social in its bearings, but no one of these matters is given undue precedence."

The New York Voice

"The author of 'Forbes of Harvard' has succeeded in doing what very few writers have done. He has told a bright, clever story by means of a series of letters. Instead of describing his characters he has let them reveal themselves in their epistles."

Detroit News-Tribune

"'Forbes of Harvard' is a series of letters written by different persons, one of whom is at Harvard, and tells in an interestingly vivid way a neat and good story, sure to be read with pleasure."

Price, paper, 50 cents; cloth, $1.25.

Mrs. S. M. H. Gardner

THE FORTUNES OF MARGARET WELD.

A novel dealing with the relation of the sexes in a bold but delicate manner.

This book tells the story of a good woman who made a grave mistake. It touches our hearts like an old sorrow, and we go with Margaret on her tortuous earth journey; we partake of her ambitions and her joys; we know the bitterness of her portion, and we, too, catch glimpses and feel somewhat at the last of her serene peace. A lofty purpose runs throughout the pages. A just tribute is indirectly paid to the Quakers, the only sect who having power never persecuted; the people who made the only treaty that was never sworn to and yet never broken. The world will be better for this book.

For sale by all newsdealers, or sent postpaid by
Arena Publishing Co., Boston, Mass.

A New Book of Social Thought. JUST PUBLISHED.

Price, paper, 25 *cents; cloth,* $1.00.

B. O. Flower

The New Time : A Plea for the Union of the Moral Forces for Practical Progress.

The Social Factors at Work in the Ascent of Man

This new work, by the author of "Civilization's Inferno," deals with practical methods for the reform of specific social evils. The writer does not bind together a mere bundle of social speculations, that would seem to many to have only a remote and abstract relevance to everyday life. He deals with facts within every one's knowledge. "The New Time" brings its matter directly home to every man's bosom and business — following Bacon's prescription.

It is published especially to meet the wants of those who wish to apply themselves to and interest their friends in the various branches of educational and social effort comprised in the platform of the National Union for Practical Progress; but, from its wide sweep of all the factors in the social problem, it will also serve to introduce many readers to a general consideration of the newer social thinking.

Price, paper, 50 *cents; cloth,* $1.00.

Rev. Minot J. Savage

The Irrepressible Conflict between Two World=Theories.

A New World, a New God, a New Humanity ·

Five lectures dealing with Christianity and evolutionary thought, to which is added " The Inevitable Surrender of Orthodoxy." By the famous Unitarian divine, advanced thinker and author of " Psychics : Facts and Theories." Mr. Savage stands in the van of the progress of moral, humane and rational ideas of human society and religion. which must be inextricably commingled in the new thinking, and a stronger word for moral and intellectual freedom has never been written than " The Irrepressible

The New Religious Thinking deals only with Verities

Conflict." We are now going through the greatest revolution of thought the world has ever seen. It means nothing less than a new universe, a new God, a new man, a new destiny.

For sale by all newsdealers or sent postpaid by
Arena Publishing Co., Boston, Mass.

Published only in cloth; price, $1.50.

Marion D. Shutter, D. D.

Wit and Humor of the Bible.

A literary study. Many writers have written instructive commentaries upon the pathos and sublimity of the Bible, but the literary elements comprised in the title of this interesting and revealing work have rarely been mentioned. Dr. Shutter has here entered into a field which before was untraversed. This side of sacred literature has been long neglected, probably because in so many minds wit and humor are somehow associated with mere ribaldry and irreverence. This is a grave mistake. Wit and humor are too fine, and have their origin in emotions too human and ennobling, to serve the purposes of coarse and mean, degraded natures. In human nature, the sources of laughter and tears lie close together; we need not, therefore, be surprised to find wit and humor in the Bible, in which every human passion is mirrored, in which the whole philosophy of life is to be found, with some consolation and sympathy for every mood of humanity. This book of Dr. Shutter's is the work of one who loves and knows the Great Book thoroughly and reverently.

Wit and Humor are sometimes confused with Buffoonery. They, however, are to be found in the highest works only, and they are subtly present in the highest

Cloth. Price, post-paid, $1.25.

Thomas Alexander Hyde

Christ the Orator : or, Never Man Spake Like This Man.

This brilliant work, the only one of its kind which has been given to the world, is a monograph upon the third side of Christ's nature — the expressional. The Rev. Thomas Alexander Hyde, the author, is a vivid and vigorous thinker, and before the publication of this book, which has made his name as familiar in the religious world as that of any contemporary religious teacher, he had made a reputation as the author of "The Natural System of Elocution and Oratory." "Christ the Orator" has already awakened widespread interest, and received high endorsement from leading editors, preachers, scholars and thoughtful laymen everywhere, representing every phase of Christian thought. Its earnest spirit, sympathetic and finished style and lofty purpose, render it a welcome guest in every family.

Mr. Hyde is a vivid writer and a vigorous thinker. His mind evidently does not run in the old theological grooves, though we conclude that he is sufficiently conservative. His attempt to prove Christ an orator is at least unique. His book is suggestive, full of bright and beautiful sayings, and is quite worth a careful reading. — *New York Herald.*

For sale by all newsdealers, or sent postpaid by
　　　　　　　　　Arena Publishing Co., Boston, Mass.

Price, paper, 50 cents ; cloth, $1.50.

The World's Congress of Religions.

A Remarkable Volume showing the Identity of all Religions in the Creeds

To meet the general demand, the Arena Publishing Company has, with the consent of the Parliament Publishing Company, issued this popular work, which gives the proceedings of the opening and closing sessions of the council *verbatim*, thus giving the reader a perfect picture of one of the most unique spectacles man has ever witnessed — a picture in which the representatives of earth's great religions united in welcome greeting and loving farewell. These two great gatherings are given *verbatim*, while in twenty-nine interesting chapters are given absolutely *verbatim* reports of the greatest and most representative papers or addresses which were delivered — the papers which most clearly set forth the views, aims and mission of the great faiths, and which are immensely valuable as contributions to the present literature of the world. It is important to remember that these addresses are in full and exactly as given. An impressive introduction has been written for this volume by Rev. Minot J. Savage.

Price, paper, 50 cents ; cloth, $1.25.

Rev. S. Weil

The Religion of the Future.

Comfort and Hope from beyond the Bourne

A Book for Sincere and Earnest Sceptics

The Higher Life Here and Now

This is a work of great value, written by one of the keenest, most powerful and most truly religious minds of the day. It is particularly a work which should be put into the hands of those who have freed themselves from the dogmas of orthodoxy and from the dogmas of materialistic science. It is a profoundly religious book. It demonstrates most indisputably to the unbiased mind the existence of a moral as well as a material cosmos. The book is addressed principally to sceptics who are seeking after truth. "The Religion of the Future" deals with that something lying behind the sympathy and interaction of mind and body at which natural science stops. It brings forward *data* to prove that this arbitrary invalidating of modern science is itself invalid.

This book starts with the axiom that the mental world is the realm of cause, of which the material world is the evanescent effect — that there is a " Power not ourselves which makes for righteousness." The chapters reveal a new method in psychic and spiritual research.

For sale by all newsdealers or sent postpaid by
Arena Publishing Co., Boston, Mass.

www.ingramcontent.com/pod-product-compliance
Lightning Source LLC
Chambersburg PA
CBHW021110020726
47500CB00003B/692